The Black Spider

Jeremias Gotthelf

Translated by H.M. Waidson

ONEWORLD
CLASSICS

ONEWORLD CLASSICS LTD
London House
243-253 Lower Mortlake Road
Richmond
Surrey TW9 2LL
United Kingdom

The Black Spider first published in 1842

This translation first published by John Calder (Publishers) Ltd in 1958
Reprinted by John Calder (Publishers) Ltd in 1980
First published in the USA in 1980 by Riverrun Press Inc.
This edition first published by Oneworld Classics Limited in 2009
Translation © John Calder (Publishers) Limited, 1958, 1980
Reprinted 2010, 2011

Front cover image © Getty Images

Printed in Great Britain by CPI Cox & Wyman

ISBN: 978-1-84749-108-4

Contents

Introduction

JEREMIAS GOTTHELF was the pseudonym by which the Swiss pastor Albert Bitzius, who died in 1854, was known as a writer of prose fiction. When his first novel *Der Bauernspiegel* (*The Peasants' Mirror*) appeared, he was thirty-nine years old, a married man with three children, and Protestant minister in the quiet village of Lützelflüh, some twenty miles to the east of Berne. His was, or appeared to be, essentially a practical temperament. He was indifferent to theoretical theology, and saw religion as something to be experienced and to be lived. Keenly interested in education, social welfare and politics, settled and happy in his family life, with a first-hand intimate knowledge of the farming community in which he worked, it might seem strange that he should turn to novel-writing and, after the publication of his first novel, pour out during the next sixteen years a varied succession of imaginative writings with a power and fluency that only ceased with his death. A man of immense vitality, he continued to be pastor of his large and scattered parish as well as to be an educationist and free-lance journalist during these years, when he wrote his twelve long novels and some forty shorter tales, and in addition one extensive novel fragment, some essays and briefer works. In a letter of December 1838, Gotthelf describes the breakthrough of his creative writing in the following terms:

Thus I was hemmed in and kept down on all sides, I could express myself nowhere in free action. I couldn't even tire myself out riding, and if I had been able to go riding every other day, I should never have written. You must realize now that a wild life was moving within me of which no one suspected the existence, and if a few expressions forced their way out of my mouth, they were taken as mere insolent words. This life had either to consume itself or to break forth in some way or other. It did so in writing. And people naturally don't realize that it is indeed a regular breaking-out of a long pent-up force, like the bursting-forth of a mountain lake. Such a lake bursts out in wild floods until it finds its own path, and sweeps mud and rocks along in its wild flight. Then it gets cleaner, and may become quite a pretty little stream. My writing too has broken its own path in the same way, a wild hitting-out in all directions where I have been constricted, in order to make space for myself. How I came to writing was on the one hand an instinctive compulsion, on the other hand I really had to write like that if I wanted to make any impression on the people.

When first published in 1842, *Die schwarze Spinne* (*The Black Spider*) aroused relatively little interest; the novel *Uli der Knecht* (*Uli the Farmhand*), which had appeared a year earlier, with its realism, humour and contemporary setting, was the work by which Gotthelf was first to become at all generally known outside Switzerland. It was not until the twentieth century that *The Black Spider* became the most widely read of its author's works. In 1949, Thomas Mann wrote that there was scarcely a work in world literature that he admired more than *The Black Spider*, and its position as one of the outstanding examples of narrative fiction in the German language is now generally recognized. Perhaps the psychological theories of Freud and Jung and the nightmare fantasies of Kafka had to be absorbed before the European imagination was ready for Gotthelf's *The Black Spider*.

The story opens idyllically, a conscious idealization of the peasant-farming way of life. The christening celebration in a farmer's family would be a homely scene of a type in which Gotthelf must frequently have taken part. Indeed the farm itself was about ten miles from Gotthelf's house and church at Lützelflüh, and the present Hornbachhof near Wasen is built on the site of the farm which he knew. The little valley of the river Grüne, with its darker patches of forest mingled with the brighter colours of the cultivated land and the scattered red-roofed farmsteads, presents a friendly, peaceful atmosphere now, as no doubt in Gotthelf's day. It is not an Alpine landscape; to the north can be seen the blue line of the Jura, and from vantage points in the district the peaks of the Bernese Oberland are on a clear day distantly visible to the south. But the valley itself is enclosed by green hills rather than high, rocky mountains. The localities named in the tale are not fictitious. The Bärhegenhubel is a hilltop some 770 feet above the valley. It is about three miles to the east of Sumiswald, with its "Bear" Inn and round table, and its nearby Kilchstalden, or "church slope"; the tree-clad Münneberg rises a little further beyond to the west of the village.

The humour and everyday realism of the framing narrative are more typical of Gotthelf's writing generally than is the legend of the black spider which forms the central interest of the tale. At one time Gotthelf planned to write a connected cycle of legendary-historical stories which should form a sequence of pictures from the Bernese past. This plan was never carried out, but a number of individual tales on these themes were written, of which *The Black Spider* is the best. This is a plague legend, and it is known that the valley was ravaged by plague in 1434. The spider theme is linked with motifs from ancient myth – the cheating of the Devil, human sacrifice, the imprisonment of the demon within a beam of wood, and others – which stretch back from legendary material of Bernese origin to remote manifestations. Hans von Stoffeln, the tyrannical knight whose harshness drives his shifty and hapless peasants into the fateful pact that precipitates the plague, was master of Sumiswald from 1512 to 1527; the historical figure, however, was known as a generous ruler, and he is in fact commemorated in one of the windows of Sumiswald Church. The Teutonic Order to which he belonged was in control of this district from 1285 to 1698, when the Sumiswald area passed into the charge of the canton of Berne. At the time of the first and more important of the two legendary narratives which are related at the christening celebration, the Order was an important military and colonizing organization, though by the seventeenth century, when the second visitation of the spider takes place, it was without authority in these lands and on the verge of disintegration. Two narratives of a historical-legendary character are thus enclosed within the framework of the Ascension Sunday christening celebration, and the unifying theme of the whole work is the baptism of children. In the legends the onslaught of the plague is described with a combination of realism and fantasy that brings myth into daily life as the battle between good and evil. Throughout the tale we are conscious of the presentation of the divine and the diabolic as co-existent with the material and human world.

Gotthelf was essentially a spontaneous and original writer, owing little to literary traditions or fashions. Echoes of the Bible are more easily discernible than any other reading influences. He wrote in a German style that was unmistakably his, colloquial, racy and shot through with local Swiss idioms, and yet at the same time massive and rocklike, capable of visionary sweep and power. The writing in *The Black Spider* often gives a sense of being written in a fury of impetuosity which is careless of conventional grammar and syntax; Gotthelf is, as it were, creating his own language and style as well as his own characters and action.

The version that follows is based on my edition of the German text, which was revised from the original manuscript now in the archives of the Stadt- und Hochschulbibliothek in Berne. For further information about this story the reader is referred to this edition (Jeremias Gotthelf, *Die schwarze Spinne*, Oxford: Blackwell, 1956) and for a fuller account of Gotthelf's life and works to my study *Jeremias Gotthelf: An Introduction to the Swiss Novelist* (Oxford: Blackwell, 1953).

– H.M. Waidson

Chronology

1797	Albert Bitzius born at Murten, now in Canton Fribourg, Switzerland.
1798	French occupation of Switzerland.
1805	The Bitzius family move to Utzenstorf, Canton Berne.
1815	Congress of Vienna and establishment of a restored federal constitution in Switzerland.
1815–20	Student of theology at Berne.
1821–22	Student at Göttingen.
1822–32	Curate at Utzenstorf, Herzogenbuchsee, Berne and Lützelflüh.
1832–54	Pastor of Lützelflüh.
1833	Marriage to Henriette Zeender.
1834	Birth of Henriette Bitzius, Gotthelf's eldest child.
1835	Birth of Albert Bitzius, Gotthelf's son.
1837	Birth of Cécile Bitzius, Gotthelf's younger daughter. *Der Bauernspiegel* (novel).
1838–39	*Leiden und Freuden eines Schulmeisters* (novel).
1841	*Wie Uli der Knecht glücklich wird* (novel).
1842	*Die schwarze Spinne* (tale).
1843	*Elsi, die seltsame Magd* (tale).
1843–44	*Geld und Geist* (novel).
1843–44	*Anne Bäbi Jowäger* (novel).
1845	*Der Geldstag* (novel).
1846–47	*Jakobs Wanderungen durch die Schweiz* (novel).
1847	*Käthi die Grossmutter* (novel). Sonderbund war, civil war in Switzerland.

The Black Spider

THE SUN ROSE OVER THE HILLS, shone with clear majesty down into a friendly, narrow valley and awakened to joyful consciousness the beings who are created to enjoy the sunlight of their life. From the sun-gilt forest's edge the thrush burst forth in her morning song, while between sparkling flowers in dew-laden grass the yearning quail could be heard joining in with its love-song; above dark pine tops eager crows were performing their nuptial dance or cawing delicate cradle songs over the thorny beds of their fledgeless young.

In the middle of the sun-drenched hillside nature had placed a fertile, sheltered, level piece of ground; here stood a fine house, stately and shining, surrounded by a splendid orchard, where a few tall apple trees were still displaying their finery of late blossom; the luxuriant grass, which was watered by the fountain near the house, was in part still standing, though some of it had already found its way to the fodder store. About the house there lay a Sunday brightness which was not of the type that can be produced on a Saturday evening in the half-light with a few sweeps of the broom, but which rather testified to a valuable heritage of traditional cleanliness which has to be cherished daily, like a family's reputation, tarnished as this may become in one single hour by marks that remain, like bloodstains, indelible from generation to generation, making a mockery of all attempts to whitewash them.

Not for nothing did the earth built by God's hand and the house built by man's hand gleam in purest adornment; today, a festal holiday, a star in the blue sky shone forth upon them both. It was the day on which the Son had returned to the

Father to bear witness that the heavenly ladder is still standing, where angels go up and down, and the soul of man too, when it wrenches itself from the body – that is, if its salvation and purpose have been with the Father above and not here below on earth – it was the day on which the whole plant world grows closer towards heaven, blooming in luxuriant plenty as an annually recurring symbol to man of his own destiny. Over the hills came a wonderful sound; no one knew where it came from, it sounded as if from all sides; it came from the churches in the far valleys beyond; from there the bells were bringing the message that God's temples are open to all whose hearts are open to the voice of their God.

Around the fine house there was lively movement. Near the fountain horses were being combed with special care, dignified matrons, with their spirited colts darting around them; in the broad trough cows were quenching their thirst, looking about them in a comfortable manner, and twice the farmer's lad had to use shovel and broom because he had not removed the traces of their well-being cleanly enough. Well-set maids were vigorously washing their ruddy faces with a handy face cloth, while their hair was twisted into two bunches over their ears; or with bustling industry they were carrying water through the open door; and in mighty puffs a dark column of smoke from the short chimney rose straight and high, up into the clear air.

Slowly the grandfather, a bent figure, was walking with his stick round the outside of the house, watching silently the doings of the farm servants and the maids; now he would stroke one of the horses, or again restrain a cow in her clumsy playfulness, or point out to the careless farmer's boy wisps of straw still lying forgotten here and there, while taking his flint and steel assiduously out of the deep pocket of his long waistcoat in order to light his pipe again, which he enjoyed so much in the morning in spite of the fact that it did not draw well.

The grandmother was sitting on a clean-swept bench in front of the house near the door, cutting fine bread into a large basin, every piece sliced thin and just the right size, not carelessly as cooks or maids would do it, who often hack off pieces big enough to choke a whale. Proud, well-fed hens and beautiful doves were quarrelling over the crumbs at her feet, and if a shy little dove did not get its share, the grandmother threw it a piece all to itself, consoling it with friendly words for the want of sense and the impetuosity of the others.

Inside in the big, clean kitchen a huge fire of pine wood was crackling; in a big pan could be heard the popping of coffee beans which a stately-looking woman was stirring around with a wooden ladle, while nearby the coffee mill was grinding between the knees of a freshly washed maid; but standing by the open door of the living room was a beautiful, rather pale woman with an open coffee sack in her hand, and she said, "Look, midwife, don't roast the coffee so black today, or else they might think I wanted to be stingy with it. The godfather's wife is really awfully suspicious and always makes the worst of everything anybody does. Half a pound or so is neither here nor there on a day like this. Oh, and don't forget to have the mulled wine ready at the right time. Grandfather wouldn't think it was a christening if we didn't set the godparents up with some mulled wine before they went to church. Don't be stingy about what's to go in it, do you hear? Over there in the dish on the kitchen dresser you'll find saffron and cinnamon, the sugar's on the table here, and take at least half as much wine again as you think is enough; at a christening there's never any need to worry that things won't get used up."

We hear that there is to be a christening in the house today, and the midwife delivers the food and drink as cleverly as she delivered the baby at an earlier stage, but she will have to hurry if she is to be ready in time and to cook at the simple fireplace everything demanded by custom.

A firmly built man came up from the cellar with a mighty piece of cheese in his hand, picked up from the gleaming kitchen dresser the first plate he could find, placed the cheese on it and was going to carry it into the living room to put on the brown walnut table. "But Benz, Benz," the beautiful, pale woman exclaimed, "how they'd laugh, if we couldn't find a better plate than this at the christening!" And she went to the gleaming cherry-wood china cupboard where the proud ornaments of the house were displayed behind the glass windows. There she took up a beautiful blue-rimmed plate with a great bunch of flowers in the middle which was surrounded by ingenious legends, such as:

Take heed, O man:
A pound of butter costs three batzen.

God is gracious to man,
But I live on good grassland.

In hell it's hot,
And the potter has to work hard.

The cow eats grass;
Man ends in the grave.

Next to the cheese she placed a huge cake, that peculiar Bernese confection, coiled like the women's plaits, beautifully brown and yellow, baked with best flour, eggs and butter, as large as a one-year-old child and weighing almost as much; and on either side she placed two more plates. Piled up on them lay appetizing fritters, yeast cakes on the one plate, pancakes on the other. Thick, warm cream was standing on the oven, covered up in a jug with lovely flowers patterned on it, and in the glistening three-legged can with its yellow lid the coffee was bubbling. In this way a breakfast was awaiting the godparents, when they should arrive, of a sort that princes seldom have and no peasant farmers in the world except the Bernese. Thousands of English people go rushing through Switzerland, but never has one of the jaded lords or one of the stiff-legged ladies been presented with a breakfast like this.

"If only they'd come soon, it's all waiting," the midwife sighed. "Anyway, it'll be a good time before they're all ready and everybody's had what they want, and the pastor is awfully punctual and ticks you off sharply if you're not there at the right time."

"Grandfather never allows the pram to be taken," the young wife said. "He believes that a child which is not carried to its christening, but is led on wheels, will grow up lazy and never learn to use its legs properly its whole life through. If only the grandmother were here, she'll hold us up longest, the godfathers make shorter work of things, and if the worst came to the worst they could always hurry along behind." Anxiety about the godparents spread through the whole house. "Aren't they coming yet?" could be heard everywhere; from all corners of the house faces peered out for them, and the dog barked for all it was worth, as if it was trying to summon them too. But the grandmother said, "It used not to be like this in the old days; then you knew that you had to get up at the right time on such a day and the pastor wouldn't wait for anybody."

Finally, the farmer's boy rushed into the kitchen with the news that the godmother was coming.

She came bathed in sweat and loaded up as if she were the Christ child going to give the New Year presents. In one hand she had the black strings of a large, flower-patterned holdall in which was a big Bernese cake wrapped in a fine white cloth, a present for the young mother. In the other hand she was carrying a second bag, and in this there was a garment for the child as well as a few articles for her own use, in particular, fine white stockings; and under the one arm she had something else, a cardboard box which contained her wreath and her laced cap with its wonderful black silk hair trimmings. Joyfully the greeting of "Welcome in God's name" was given her from all sides, and she scarcely had time to put down one of her parcels so that she could free her own hand to meet the hands stretched towards her in friendly welcome. From all directions helpful hands reached for her burdens, and there was the young wife standing by the door, and so a new series of greetings began, until the midwife summoned them into the living room: they could surely say to each other inside there what custom demanded on such an occasion.

And with neat gestures the midwife placed the godmother at the table, and the young wife came with the coffee, even though the godmother refused and asserted that she had already had some. Her father's sister wouldn't let her leave the house without having something to eat, that was bad for young girls, she said. But after all her aunt was getting old now, and the maids didn't like getting up early either, that was why she was so late; if it had been left to her, she would have been here long ago. Thick cream was poured into the coffee, and although the godmother protested and said she did not like it, the wife threw a lump of sugar in all the same. For a long time the godmother would not have it that the Bernese cake should be cut for her, but then she had to let a good-sized piece be placed in front of her and to eat it. She didn't want any cheese, she said; she didn't need it a bit. The wife said she believed it was made from skimmed milk and did not think much to it on that account, and the godmother had to give in. But she didn't want any fritters, she said; she just wouldn't know where to find room for them. It was only that she believed they were not clean and she was used to better quality, was the answer she finally received. What else could she do except eat fritters? While she was being pressed to eat in all kinds of ways, she had drunk her first cup of coffee in short measured sips, and now a real dispute started. The godmother turned the cup upside down and claimed that she had no more room for any further good things, saying people should leave her in peace, or else, what is more, she would have to refuse in even stronger language. Then the wife said she was really sorry that she didn't like the coffee, she had ordered the midwife most emphatically to make it as good as possible, it really wasn't her fault that it was so bad that nobody wanted to drink it, and there surely couldn't be anything wrong with the cream either, she had taken it off the milk in a way she certainly didn't every day. What was the poor godmother to do except to let them pour her another cup?

For some time now the midwife had been hovering around impatiently, and at last she could restrain herself no longer, but said, "If there's anything you'd like me to do for you, just tell me, I've got time for it!"

"Oh, don't be rushing us!" the wife said.

The poor godmother, however, who was steaming like a kettle, took the hint, dispatched the hot coffee as quickly as possible, and said, during the pauses forced on her by the burning drink, "I should have been ready long ago, if I hadn't had to take more than I can get down me, but I'm coming now."

She got up, unpacked her bags, handed over the Bernese cake, the infant's garment and the godmother's own present – a shining neuthaler coin, wrapped up in a beautifully painted piece of paper which had a christening text on it – and made many an apology because everything was not as good as it might be. But the mother interrupted with many an exclamation that that really wasn't the way to go about it, putting yourself to so much expense that they almost felt they couldn't accept it; and if they'd known it, they wouldn't have thought of asking her to be godmother in the first place.

Now the girl too set to work, assisted by the midwife and the lady of the house, and did her utmost to be a beautiful godmother, from shoes and stockings up to the little wreath on top of the precious lace cap. The business took its time in spite of the midwife's impatience, and the godmother kept on finding something that was not as it should be, now one thing, and now another was not in the right place. Then the grandmother came in and said, "But I want to come in as well and see how lovely our godmother is." At the same time she let out that the church bells were ringing for the second time, and that both godfathers were in the outer room.

Indeed the two godfathers, an older man and a young man, were sitting outside, scorning the newfangled coffee, which they could have any day, in favour of the steaming mulled wine, this old-fashioned but good Bernese soup, consisting of wine, toasted bread, eggs, sugar, cinnamon and saffron, that equally old-fashioned spice which has to be present at a christening feast in the soup, in the first course after the soup and in the sweetened tea. They were enjoying it, and the older godfather, who was called "Cousin", made all sorts of jokes with the father of the newborn child and said to him that they didn't want to spare him today, and judging from the mulled wine he didn't begrudge it them, and nothing had been stinted in making it, you could see that he must have given his four-gallon sack to the messenger last Tuesday to fetch his saffron from Berne. When they did not know what the cousin meant by this, he said that a little while back his neighbour had had to have a christening and had given the messenger a large sack and six kreuzer with the request to bring him in this sack six centimes' worth of the yellow powder, a quart or a bit over, that stuff you have to have in everything at christenings, his womenfolk seemed to want it that way.

Then the godmother entered like a young morning sun and was greeted by the two godfathers and brought to the table and a big dishful of mulled wine put in front of her, and she was to get that inside her, she'd got time enough while the baby was being put straight. The poor lass resisted with might and main, and asserted that she had had enough to eat to last her for days, she really couldn't even breathe any more. But it was no use. Old folk and young were urging her, both seriously and in fun, until she picked up the spoon and, strangely enough, one spoonful after another found its way down. Now, however, the midwife appeared again, this time with the baby beautifully wrapped in his swaddling clothes, and she put his embroidered cap with its pink silk ribbon on him, wrapped him in the lovely quilt, popped the sweetened dummy into his little mouth and said that she didn't want to keep anybody waiting and had thought she'd get everything ready so that they could start whenever they wanted. Everyone stood round the baby and made complimentary remarks about it, and he was indeed a bonny little boy. The mother was pleased at the praise and said, "I should have liked to come to church too and help to recommend the child to God's care; for if you're there yourself when the baby is being christened, you can think better about what you've promised. Besides, it's such a nuisance if I'm not allowed outside the house for a whole week, especially now when we've got our hands full with the planting." But the grandmother said it hadn't got quite that far, that her daughter-in-law had to go to be churched within the first week like a poor woman, and the midwife added that she didn't like it at all when young women went with the children to christening. They were always afraid of something going wrong at home, didn't have the proper spirit in church, and on the way home they were in too much of a hurry, so that nothing should be missed, then they got too hot and sometimes became really ill and even died.

Then the godmother took the baby in his coverlet in her arms, and the midwife laid the beautiful white christening cloth with black tassles at the corners over the child, being careful to avoid the lovely bunch of flowers on the godmother's breast, and said, "Go on now, in God's holy name!" And the grandmother put her hands together and quietly said an ardent prayer of blessing. The mother, however, accompanied the procession as far as the door and said, "My little boy, my little boy, now I shan't be seeing you for three whole hours. I don't know how I can stand it!" And at once tears came to her eyes, quickly she wiped them away with her apron and went back into the house.

With rapid steps the godmother walked down the slope along the way to the church, bearing the fine child in her strong arms, behind her the two godfathers, the father and the grandfather, none of whom thought of relieving the godmother of her burden, although the younger godfather was wearing on his hat a good sprig of may, the sign that he was a bachelor, and in his eyes was a sparkle of something like approval of the godmother, hidden though this was behind an appearance of great nonchalance.

The grandfather informed everybody how terrible the weather had been when he himself had been carried to church to be christened, and how the churchgoers had hardly believed they would escape with their lives from the hail and lightning. Later on people had made all kinds of prophecies to him on account of this weather, some predicting a terrible death, others great fortune in war; but things had gone quietly for him just as they had for everybody else, and now that he was seventy-five he would neither die an early death nor have great fortune in war.

They had gone more than halfway when the maid came running after them; she had the duty of carrying the baby back home as soon as he had been christened, while relatives and godparents stayed behind, according to the grand old custom, in order to listen to the sermon. The maid had not spared any efforts so that she too might look beautiful. This considerable labour had made her late, and now she wanted to relieve the godmother of the baby; but the godmother would not allow this, however much she was pressed. This was too good an opportunity to show the handsome, unmarried godfather how strong her arms were and how much they could put up with. For a real peasant farmer strong arms on a woman are much more acceptable than delicate, miserable little sticks of arms that every north wind can blow apart if it sets its mind to it; a mother's strong arms have been the salvation of many children whose father has died, when the mother has to rule the family alone and must lift unaided the cart of housekeeping out of all the potholes in which it might get stuck.

But all at once it is as if somebody is holding the strong godmother back by her plaits or giving her a blow on the head, she actually recoils, gives the maid the child, then stays behind and pretends that she has to see to her garter. Then she catches up, attaches herself to the men, mixes in their conversations, tries to interrupt the grandfather and distract him, now with this, now with that, from the subject which he has taken up. He, however, holds firmly on to his subject, as old people usually do, and imperturbably takes up afresh the broken thread of his narrative. Now she makes up to the father of the child and tries through all sorts of questions to lead him into private conversation; yet he is monosyllabic and keeps on letting the conversation drop. Perhaps he has his own thoughts, as every father should, when his child, and what is more the first boy, is being taken to be christened. The nearer they came to the church, the more people joined to the procession, some were already waiting by the wayside with their psalters in their hands, others were leaping more hurriedly down the narrow footpaths, and they came into the village like a great, solemn procession.

Next to the church was the inn, for these two institutions so often stand close to one another, sharing joy and suffering together, and what is more, in all honour. There a halt was made, the baby was changed, and the father ordered three litres of wine, although everyone protested that he shouldn't do it, they'd only just had all the heart could desire, and they wanted nothing, great or small. Even so, once the wine was there, they all drank, especially the maid; she presumably thought she had to drink wine whenever anybody offered it to her, and that wouldn't happen often from one year's end to the next. Only the godmother could not be persuaded to touch a drop, in spite of her being pressed as if they would never stop, until the innkeeper's wife said they ought not to force her, the girl was becoming visibly paler, and Hoffmann's Drops would do her more good than wine. But the godmother did not want anything like that, scarcely wanted even a glass of wine, in the end had to allow a few drops from a bottle of smelling salts to be shaken onto her handkerchief, attracted in her innocence many a suspicious glance and could not justify herself or say what she needed. The godmother was suffering from a ghastly fear and could not say anything about it. Nobody had told her what name the baby was to have, and according to old custom it is the godmother's duty to whisper the name to the pastor on handing the child over to him, since the pastor could easily confuse the names that have been registered with him if there are many children to be baptized.

In their hurry about the many things that had to be done and in their fear of coming too late, they had forgotten to inform her of the name, and her father's sister, her aunt, had once and for all strictly forbidden her to ask what the name was, unless she really wanted to make a child unhappy; for as soon as a godmother asked about a child's name, this child would become inquisitive for his whole life. Thus she did not know the child's name, might not ask about it, and if the pastor had also forgotten it and asked what it was loudly in public or else made a mistake and christened the boy Magdalena or Barbara, how people would laugh and what a humiliation this would be her whole life through! This appeared to her as ever more terrible; the strong girl's legs trembled like bean plants in the wind, and the sweat poured off her pale face in streams.

At this point the innkeeper's wife urged them to depart if they wanted to avoid being hauled over the coals by the pastor; but to the godmother she said, "You'll never go through with it, lass, you're as white as a newly washed shirt."

That was from running, the godmother asserted, it would get better again when she came into the fresh air. But it would not get better: in church all the people looked quite black to her, and now the baby began to scream with an increasingly murderous yell. The poor godmother began to rock him in her arms, and the louder he cried, the more vigorously she rocked him, so that the petals scattered from the flowers on her breast. Her breast felt more constricted and heavier, and her breathing could be heard loud. The higher her breast rose, the higher the child flew up in her arms, and the higher he flew, the louder he screamed, and the louder he screamed, the more forcefully the pastor read the prayers. The voices actually resounded against the walls, and the godmother no longer knew where she was; there was a whistling and roaring around her like the waves of the sea, and the church danced around with her in the air. At last the pastor said "Amen", and now the terrible moment had come; now it was to be decided whether she was to become a laughing stock for children and grandchildren; now she had to take off the covering, give the child to the pastor and whisper the name into his right ear. She removed the cloth, though trembling and shaking, handed over the child, and the pastor took him, did not look at her, did not ask her with sharp eyes, dipped his hand in the water, wetted the forehead of the suddenly silent child and did not christen him a Magdalena or a Barbara, but a Hans Uli, an honest-to-goodness real-life Hans Uli.

At that the godmother felt not only as if all the Emmental hills were falling off her heart, but sun, moon and stars too, and as if someone were carrying her from a fiery furnace into a cool bath; but all through the sermon her limbs trembled and would not be still again. The pastor preached very finely and penetratingly, all about man's life being nothing more nor less than an ascension towards heaven; but the godmother could not arrive at a proper devotional state of mind, and by the time they left the church she had already forgotten the text. She could hardly wait to reveal her secret fear and the reason for her pale face. There was a lot of laughter, and she had to hear many a joke about inquisitiveness, and how scared the womenfolk were of this, and how all the same they saw to it that their daughters became inquisitive, although they left the boys out of it. She really needn't have worried about asking.

Soon, however, fine fields of oats and plantations of flax and the magnificent growth in meadows and fields came to be noticed and attracted everyone's attention. They found a number of reasons for going slowly and standing still, but by the time they arrived home the beautiful May sun, which was higher in the sky now, had made them all feel warm, and a glass of cool wine did everybody good, however much they resisted it. Then they sat down in front of the house, while in the kitchen busy hands were at work and the fire was crackling mightily. The midwife was gleaming like one of the three men from the fiery furnace. Already before eleven o'clock came a summons to the meal, but only for the servants, who were given their food first, and in ample quantity of course, but all the same one was glad when the servants were out of the way.

The conversation of those sitting in front of the house flowed rather slowly, but it did not dry up completely; before a meal preoccupation with the stomach disturbs the thoughts of the soul, but nobody is pleased to reveal this inner state, rather it is cloaked over with slow words on trivial subjects. It was already past midday when the midwife appeared at the door with flaming face, though her apron was still spotless, and brought the news, welcome to all, that they could eat if they were all there. But most of the guests were still missing, and the messengers who had already been sent out after them earlier returned, like the servants in the Gospel, with all kinds of information, with the distinction, however, that actually all were willing to come, only not just now; the one had ordered workmen to come, the other farm servants, and the third still had to go off somewhere – but they weren't to wait for them, but just to get on with the business. It was soon agreed to follow this exhortation, for if you were going to wait for everyone, it was said, it would drag out until the moon rose; it is true that the midwife growled in passing that there was nothing sillier than keeping people waiting, when in fact everybody would like to be there, the sooner the better in fact, so long as nobody should notice it. So you have the trouble of getting everything warmed up again, you never know whether there's enough, and you never get finished.

Although it did not take long to come to a decision about the absentees, there was a certain amount of trouble with those who were present in leading them to the living room and persuading them to sit down there, for nobody wanted to be first, at one thing any more than another. When at last they were all seated, the soup came to the table, a beautiful meat soup, coloured and spiced with saffron and so thickly covered with the beautiful white bread that the grandmother had been cutting that there was little of the soup itself visible. Now all heads were uncovered, hands were folded together, and each one prayed to himself long and earnestly to the Giver of all good gifts. Only then did they slowly take up their metal spoons, and after wiping these on the beautiful, fine tablecloth they applied themselves to the soup, and many a wish could be heard that they could ask for no more than this, that they might have such a good soup every day. When they had finished their soup, they again wiped their spoons on the tablecloth; the Bernese cake was handed round, and everybody cut themselves a piece, at the same time observing that the first meat course was being served up, which consisted of meat in saffron broth – mutton, brains and liver prepared in vinegar. When this course had been dealt with, after people had helped themselves in a slow and deliberate manner, the beef was brought in, both fresh meat and salted meat, whichever one might fancy, piled up high in dishes; with this went dried beans, slices of dried pear, broad strips of bacon and wonderful joints from pigs that weighed three hundredweight, beautifully red and white and succulent. All this slowly took its course, and whenever a new guest arrived, the whole meal was brought on again, beginning with the soup, and each newcomer had to begin where the others had begun earlier, none was let off a single course. In between, Benz, the father of the newborn child, assiduously poured out wine from the beautiful white bottles which held more than a gallon and were richly decorated with coats of arms and mottoes. Where his arms could not reach, he transferred to others his office of cup-bearer, earnestly pressing his guests to drink and very often exhorting them: "Drink it up, that's what it's there for, to be drunk!" And whenever the midwife came in carrying a dish of food, he held out his glass to her, and others did the same too, so that things might have gone very queerly in the kitchen if she had drunk a pledge every time that one was offered her.

The younger godfather had to listen to a number of jokes to the effect that he did not know how to encourage the godmother to drink as well as he should; if he could not give toasts better than that, he would never get a wife. "Oh, Hans Uli won't want a wife," the godmother finally said; unmarried fellows these days had quite different ideas in their heads from marriage, and most of them couldn't even afford to get married now. "Huh," said Hans Uli, he wasn't so sure about that. Such slovenly creatures as most girls were nowadays made very expensive wives; most of them thought that all that was needed to make a good wife was a piece of blue silk to wrap round their heads, gloves in summer and embroidered slippers in winter. If you found that one of the cows in the cowshed was a poor specimen, that was certainly bad luck, but you could change it all the same; but if you were landed with a wife who did you out of a house and farm, that was the end of it, and you can't get rid of her. That's why it was more useful to think about other things rather than marriage and to let girls remain girls.

"Yes, yes, you're quite right," the older godfather said; he was an insignificant-looking little man in cheap clothes, but he was respected very much and called "Cousin", for he had no children, but did possess a farm of his own without a mortgage on it and 100,000 Swiss francs in capital. "Yes, you are right," he said. "Womenfolk are just no use any more. I won't say that there isn't one here or there who would do credit to a house, but such are few and far between. All they can think about is foolery and showing off; they dress up like peacocks, strut about like daft storks, and if one of them has to do half a day's work, she gets a headache that lasts three days, and spends four days lying in bed before she is herself again. When I was courting my old woman, things were different, you didn't have to fear as much as you do now that you might get, instead of a good mistress of the house, only a fool or a devil about the house."

"Now look here, godfather Uli," said the godmother who had been wanting to talk for a long time, but had not had a chance, "anyone would think that it was only in your young days that there were any decent farmers' daughters. The only thing is, you just don't know them and you don't take any notice of girls any more, which of course is quite right in an old man like you; but there are decent girls still, just as much as in the days when your old woman was still young. I don't want to blow my own trumpet, but my father has told me many a time that if I go on as I have been doing, I shall outdo my late mother yet, and she became a really famous woman. My father has never taken such fat pigs to market as last year. The butcher has often said that he'd like to see the lass who had fed those pigs. But there's plenty to complain about in young fellows today; just what on earth is wrong with them then? They can certainly smoke, sit around in the inn, wear their white hats on the slant and open their eyes as wide as city gates, hang around all the skittle games, all the shooting matches and all the loose girls, but if one of them is supposed to milk a cow or plough a field, he's had it, and if he takes a piece of timber in his hands, he behaves as stupidly as a gentleman or even a lawyer's clerk. I have often solemnly sworn that I won't have anybody as a husband unless I know for certain how I can get on with him, and even if one of them here or there may turn out to be something of a farmer, that doesn't help you to know at all what he would be like as a husband."

At this the others laughed heartily, making the girl blush as they joked with her; how long did she think that she would want to take a man on approval until she knew for certain what sort of a husband he would be?

In this way, laughing and joking, they ate a lot of meat and did not forget the pear slices either, until eventually the older godfather said that he thought that they should be contented for the time being and move away a little from the table, for your legs got quite stiff beneath the table and a pipe is never more welcome than after you've been eating meat. This counsel received general acclamation, even though the father and mother tried to persuade the guests not to leave the table; once people had moved away, there was hardly a hope of bringing them back again.

"Don't you worry, Cousin!" said the older godfather. "As soon as you put something good on the table, you'll have us all together again without much trouble, and if we stretch our legs a bit, we shall be all the more handy at tackling the food again."

The men now made the round of the cattle sheds, took a look at the hayloft to see if any of the old hay was still available, made compliments about the lush grass and stared up into the fruit trees to calculate how great the blessing of this crop might be.

The cousin made a halt beneath one of the trees that was still in bloom and said that this was as good a place as any to sit down and have a pipe, it was cool here, and as soon as the womenfolk had served up something good again, they would be near at hand. Soon they were joined by the godmother who with the other women had been inspecting the vegetable garden and the plantations. The other womenfolk came after the godmother, and one after another lowered themselves onto the grass, carefully keeping their beautiful skirts safe and clean, although their petticoats with their bright-red edging were exposed to the danger of receiving a souvenir on them from the green grass.

The tree around which the whole company was encamped stood above the house on the first gentle rise of the slope. The beautiful new house was what first caught the eye; beyond the house the glance could rove to the edge of the valley on the other side, looking over many a fine, prosperous farm, and further away over green hills and dark valleys.

"You've got a grand house there, and everything is well planned about it too," the cousin said. "Now you can really enjoy being in it, and you've got room for everything and everybody; I never could understand how anybody could put up with such a poor house when they have enough money and timber to build for themselves, as you have, for example."

"Don't tease, Cousin!" the grandfather said. "There's no cause for us to boast either about money or timber – and then, building is a grim business, you know when you start, but you never know when you're going to finish, and now one thing gets in the way, now another; every place has got something else that can go wrong."

"I like the house extremely well," one of the women said. "We too ought to have had a new house for a long time now, but we always shy off at the expense. But as soon as my husband arrives, he must have a good look at this house; it seems to me that if we could have a house like this, I should be in heaven. But all the same I would like to ask – and don't take it amiss, will you? – why ever that ugly black window post is there, just by the first window; it detracts from the appearance of the whole house."

The grandfather pulled a dubious face, drew even more vigorously at his pipe and finally said that they had run out of wood when they were building, there was nothing else just at hand, and so they had taken in their need and haste something from the old house.

"But," the woman said, "the black piece of wood was too short, apart from anything else, and there are pieces joined on top and bottom – besides, any neighbour would have been only too glad to give you a really new piece."

"Yes, we just didn't think it out better and we could not always be pestering our neighbours afresh, they had already given us a lot of help with gifts of timber and with the loan of horses and carts," the old man replied.

"Listen, Granddad," the cousin said, "don't beat about the bush, but tell the truth and give an honest account. I've already heard various rumours, but I've never yet been able to hear the truth exactly. Now would be a good time, you could entertain us so well with the story, until the women have got the roast ready – so you give us an honest account!" The grandfather still beat about the bush before he would consent, but the cousin and the womenfolk did not give way until he at last gave his promise, though nevertheless with the express reservation that he would prefer what he had to tell to remain a secret and not to go beyond the present company. A good many people would fight shy of anything like that about a house, and he would not like to be responsible in his old age for anything that might harm his own relatives.

"Every time that I look at this piece of wood," the venerable old man began, "I cannot but wonder how it all happened that people came as far as here from the distant east, where the human race is said to have originated, and found this spot in this narrow valley; I cannot but think of those who drifted here or else were driven here, and everything that they must have suffered, and who indeed they may have been. I have enquired a lot about it, but all I have been able to find out is that this district was inhabited very early in history, and indeed that Sumiswald is supposed to have been a town even before Our Lord was on earth – but that is not written down anywhere. However, we do know that a castle, where the hospital now is, stood there more than six hundred years ago, and apparently about the same time there would have been a house here too which belonged to the castle, along with a great part of the district; the house would have to pay tithes and ground rent to the castle, and compulsory labour would have to be performed as well; for the people then were held as serfs without legal rights of their own, as everybody is now as soon as he becomes an adult. People lived in widely divergent conditions in those days: quite close together there lived serfs who had the best conditions and those who were sorely and almost unbearably oppressed and were not even sure of their lives. Their circumstances depended on who their lord was at the time; these lords were very different from one another and at the same time almost absolute masters over their people; the latter had no one to whom they could make their complaint easily and effectively. Those who belonged to this castle are said to have suffered worse at times than most of those who belonged to other castles. Most of the other castles belonged to one family and were passed down from father to son; here the lord and his subjects were known to each other from youth onwards, and many a one behaved like a father to his people. Now this castle came at an early stage into the hands of the Teutonic Knights, as they were called, and the one who was in charge here was known as the district commander. These superiors changed frequently, and for a time there was somebody from Saxony, and then somebody from Swabia; consequently no sense of trust could grow, and each commander brought manners and customs with him from his own country.

In fact the knights were supposed to fight against the heathen in Poland and Prussia, and in these countries they almost accustomed themselves to the heathen way of living, treated their fellow men as if there were no God in heaven, and when they did eventually come home they continued to fancy that they were still in the heathen country and carried on with the same type of life here. Those who preferred to sit in the shade and enjoy themselves rather than to fight bloodily in grim, desert country, or those who had to nurse their wounds and strengthen their bodies, came to the lands which the Order (such was called the company of the knights) possessed in Germany and in Switzerland, and each of the commanders could do as he pleased. One of the worst of them is said to have been Hans von Stoffeln from Swabia, and it was under his rule that these things are said to have happened which you want to know about and which have been passed down in our family from father to son.

This man Hans von Stoffeln had the idea of building a great castle up over there on the Bärhegenhubel; the castle stood on the spot where in stormy weather you can even now still see the spirits of the castle displaying their treasures. Usually the knights built their castles near the roads, just as today inns are built by the roadside; in both cases it is a question of being able to plunder the people better, though in different ways, admittedly. But why the knight wanted to have a castle up there on the wild, bare hill in the midst of deserted country, we do not know; it is enough that he did want it, and the peasants who were attached to the castle had to do the building. The knight was indifferent to what work might be demanded by the season, whether it was haymaking time, harvest time or seed time. So many teams or carts had to move, so many men had to labour, and at this or that particular time the last tile had to be in place and the last nail knocked in. What is more, he insisted on every tenth sheaf of corn that was due to him and on every measure of his ground rent; he never let them have a chicken for Shrove Tuesday nor even an egg; he had no pity, and knew nothing of the needs of the poor. He spurred them on in heathen manner with blows and curses, and if anyone became tired, or was slower in his movements or wanted to rest, the bailiff would be at his back with the whip, and neither the aged nor the weak were spared. When the wild knights were up there, they enjoyed hearing the crack of the whip and playing all sorts of unpleasant tricks on the workers; if they could maliciously compel the men to double the pace of their work, they did not refrain from doing so and then took great pleasure in their fear and sweat.

At last the castle was finished, with its walls that were five yards thick; nobody knew why it was standing up there, but the peasants were glad that it really did stand, if it had to be there at all, and that the last nail was knocked in and the last tile fixed into place up on top.

They wiped the sweat from their brows, looked round their own property with dejected hearts and sighed to see to what extent the accursed building work had held them back. But there was a long summer ahead of them all the same, and God was above them; therefore they took courage and firmly grasped their ploughs, consoling their wives and children who had suffered severe hunger and for whom work appeared as yet another torment.

But scarcely had they taken their ploughs to the fields when the message came that all the peasants were to appear one evening at a specific time in the castle at Sumiswald. They were both fearful and hopeful. It was true that they had up to now experienced nothing enjoyable at the hands of the present inhabitants of the castle, but had only suffered malice and severity, but it seemed right to them that the gentry should do something for them as a reward for the unheard-of piece of forced labour which had just been accomplished; and because the peasants thought it seemed right, many of them believed their lords would think so too, and they hoped they would that evening be given a present or a remission of some other obligations.

On the evening arranged, they appeared punctually and with beating hearts, but they had to wait a long time in the courtyard of the castle where the servants could jeer at them. These servants too had been in heathen countries. What is more, it must have been the same then as it is now, when every twopenny-halfpenny gentleman's lackey thinks he has a right to look down on and be scornful of property-owning peasants.

Eventually they were summoned to the hall of the knights; in front of them the heavy door was opened; inside the darkly tanned knights sat round the heavy oak table, fierce dogs at their feet, and at their head was von Stoffeln, a fierce, powerful man who had a head like a three-litre jug, eyes like cartwheels and a beard like an old lion's mane. Then the knights laughed so that the wine slopped over their tankards and the dogs darted angrily forwards; for as soon as dogs like these see trembling, hesitant limbs they have the idea that they belong to some prey that should be hunted down. The peasants, however, did not feel confident; they thought, if only they were back home, and each tried to hide behind the other. When at last dogs and knights were silent, von Stoffeln raised his voice, and it sounded as if it came from a hundred-year-old oak: 'My castle is finished, but there is something still missing; summer is coming, and up there there is no avenue of trees to provide a shady walk. In a month you must plant an avenue for me; you must take a hundred full-grown beech trees from the Münneberg root and branch, and plant them for me on Bärhegen, and if one single beech tree is missing, I shall make you pay for it with property and life. Down below there is something to eat and drink, but the first beech must be standing on Bärhegen tomorrow.'

When one of the peasants heard something about food and drink he thought that the knight might be lenient and in a good mood, and he therefore began to talk about their work at home and their hungry wives and children, and the fact that this particular task could be better done in winter. Then the knight's head seemed to become more and more puffed out with anger, and his voice exploded like a thunderclap amid steep rocks, and he told them that if he were lenient, they were indolent. If someone in Poland was allowed to keep his bare life, he would kiss your feet with gratitude, but here they had children and cattle, a roof over their heads and cupboards to put their things in, and still they were not satisfied. 'But I will make you more obedient and more contented, as sure as I am Hans von Stoffeln, and if the hundred beech trees are not planted up there within a month, I'll have you whipped until there's not a finger's length of your skin left whole, and I'll set the dogs on your women and children.'

Then nobody dared to remonstrate further, but neither did anyone want any of the food and drink; after the angry order had been given, they pressed out to the door, and every one of them would gladly have been the first to leave, and for a long time after they had gone they were followed by the knight's voice of thunder and the laughter of the other knights, the jeering of the servants and the howling of the hounds.

When they came to a turn in the road, where they could no longer be seen from the castle, they sat down by the roadside and wept bitterly; no one had any consolation for his neighbour, and none of them had the courage for real anger, for privation and torments had extinguished their courage, so that they had no more strength left for anger, only enough for despair. They were to transport beech trees, complete with roots and branches, for a three-hour journey over rough tracks up the steep Münneberg, while close by this hill many fine beeches were growing, but these had to be left standing! Within a month the work had to be finished; they were to drag three trees each of the first two days and four trees every third day, and the hill was steep and their cattle already exhausted. And in addition to all this it was May, the month when the peasant has to work hard in his fields and may hardly leave them by day or night, if he wants to have bread and food for the winter.

While they were waiting there so disconsolately, none daring to look into the other's face to see his misery because his own distress already overwhelmed him, and none daring to take the bad news home to his wife and family, there suddenly appeared in front of them – they did not know where he had come from – the tall, lean figure of a green huntsman. A red feather was swaying on his bold cap, a little red beard blazed in his dark face, and a mouth opened between his hooked nose and pointed chin, almost invisible like a cavern beneath overhanging rocks, and uttered the question: 'What's the matter, good people, that you are sitting and moaning like this, as if to force the rocks out of the earth and the branches down from the trees?' Twice he asked thus, and twice he received no answer.

Then the green huntsman's dark face became even darker and his little red beard became even redder, so that it seemed to be crackling and sparkling like pine wood on fire; his mouth pursed itself sharply like an arrow and then opened to ask quite pleasingly and gently: 'But good people, what use is it your sitting and moaning there? You could go on howling like that till a second Flood comes or till your shrieking brings down the stars from the sky, but that's not likely to help you very much. But when somebody asks you what's wrong, somebody who means well by you and could possibly help you, you ought to answer and say something sensible instead of crying out loud – that might be more use to you.' At that an old man shook his white head of hair and replied, 'Don't take it amiss, but no huntsman can take away the cause of our weeping, and once the heart is swollen with grief, it can find words no longer.'

Then the green huntsman shook his sharp head and said, 'Father, what you say is not stupid, but that's not the way things are. You can strike anything you please, a rock or a tree, and it will utter a sound, it will lament. A man too should lament, should lament about everything, should complain to the first person he meets, for perhaps this person can help him. I am only a huntsman, but who knows whether I haven't got an efficient team of cattle at home to transport wood and stones or beech trees and pines?'

When the poor peasants heard the word 'team', it went straight to their hearts and there became a spark of hope; all eyes turned towards the huntsman, and the old man opened his mouth once more; he said it was not always right to tell the first person you met what was on your mind, but since they could tell from his words that he meant well and that he might perhaps help, they wouldn't hide anything from him. They had suffered now for more than two years from the building of the new castle, and there was not a single household in the whole community which was not in bitter distress. Now they had taken fresh breath, thinking that they would at last have their hands free for their own work, the administration had just given them the order to plant within one month by the new castle a new avenue of beech trees taken from the Münneberg. They did not know how they could accomplish this in the time with their exhausted cattle, and if they did accomplish the task, what use would it be to them? They would not then be able to plant and to sow their own fields and would have to die of starvation later, even if the hard work for the knight had not killed them before that. They were reluctant to take this news to their homes, for they did not want to pour new grief onto old misery.

Then the green huntsman made a sympathetic face, lifted up his long, thin, black hand threateningly against the castle and swore deep vengeance for such tyranny. But he would help the peasants, he said. His equipment was like none other in the country, and as many trees as they could bring to Kilchstalden, on this side of Sumiswald, he would transport from there to Bärhegen, as a favour to them and to spite the knights and for very little payment.

The poor men pricked up their ears on hearing this unexpected offer. If they could only make an agreement about the payment, they were saved, for they could bring the beech trees to Kilchstalden without neglecting their farm work on account of this task and consequently without being utterly ruined. The old man therefore said, 'Well, tell us what you require, so that we can make an agreement!' Then the green huntsman showed a cunning face; his little beard crackled, and his eyes gleamed at them like snakes' eyes, and a hideous laugh came from the two corners of his mouth as he opened his lips and said, 'As I was saying, I don't ask for much, nothing more than an unbaptized child.'

The word flashed at the men like lightning, scales fell from their eyes, and like spray in a whirlwind they scattered in different directions.

Then the green huntsman laughed out loud, so that the fish in the stream hid themselves and the birds sought cover in the thicket, and the feather swayed horribly on his hat while his little beard went up and down.

'Think it over, or see what your womenfolk have got to say about it; you'll find me here again in three nights' time!' He called after the men in flight in a sharp, resounding voice, so that the words remained fixed in their ears as arrows with barbed hooks stay stuck in flesh.

Pale and trembling in mind as in all their limbs, the men rushed home; none looked round at one of the others, not one would have turned his head round, not for everything in the world. When the men came rushing along in this scared way, like doves that have been chased by a hawk into their dovecote, they brought terror with them into all the houses, and everybody trembled fearfully to hear what news it was that had made the men stumble and hasten in such confusion.

Quivering with curiosity the womenfolk crept after the men until they had them in some quiet place where confidences could be exchanged undisturbed. There each man had to tell his wife what had been heard in the castle, and the women received the news with curses and fury; the men had to relate whom they had met and what he had proposed to them. Then nameless fear seized hold of the women, a cry of pain resounded over hills and valley, and each woman felt as if it were her own child that the ruthless huntsman had demanded. Only one woman did not cry out like the rest. This was a terribly forceful woman, who was said to have come from Lindau and who lived here on this very farm. She had wild, black eyes and had little fear of God or man. She had already been angry with the men for not refusing the knight's demands there and then; if she had been there, she'd have told him straight, she said. When she heard about the green huntsman and his offer and how the men had rushed away, she really did become angry and reviled the men for their cowardice; if they had looked the green huntsman more boldly in the face, he might perhaps have contented himself with some other payment, and as the work was to be for the castle, it would do their souls no harm if the Devil undertook it for them. She was enraged at heart because she had not been there, even if only that she could have seen the Devil himself and known what he looked like. That is why this woman did not weep, but in her fury uttered hard words against her own husband and against all the other men.

On the following day, when the cry of dismay had subsided into a quiet whimpering, the men sat together, looking for wise counsel, but finding none. At first there was talk of making a fresh request to the knight, but nobody was willing to go to make a petition, for nobody wanted to risk life and limb. One man suggested sending the women and children with their crying and moaning, but he soon became silent when the women themselves began to talk; for already in those days women were not far away when the menfolk took counsel together. The women knew of no other plan except to attempt obedience in God's name; they suggested having masses sung in order to obtain God's protection, or requesting neighbours to give them secret help by night, for their lords would not have allowed outside help openly; they thought of splitting up, the one half to work at the beech trees, while the other half should sow oats and look after the cattle. In this way they hoped with God's help to bring up to Bärhegen at least three beeches a day; nobody mentioned the green huntsman; whether anyone thought of him or not is not recorded.

They divided themselves up and prepared their tools, and when the first May morning appeared at its threshold, the men met at the Münneberg and began the work with good heart. The beeches had to be dug up in a wide circle in order to spare the roots and then lowered carefully to the ground. The morning was still not yet far advanced when three trees lay ready to be moved, for it had been decided that they should always transport three together, so that the men could help each other out with their cattle as well as with the strength of their hands. But when midday came, they still had not got the three beech trees out of the forest, and when the sun went down behind the mountains, the teams had still not gone further than Sumiswald. It was not until the next morning that they reached the foot of the hill on which the castle stood and where the beeches were to be planted. It was as if a special unlucky star had power over them. One misfortune after another befell them: harnesses snapped, carts broke, horses and oxen fell down or else refused obedience. On the second day matters became even worse. New distress inevitably brought new toil with it, the wretched folk were breathless with the unceasing labour, and still there was no beech tree up at the top, and only three trees had been transported any further than Sumiswald.

Von Stoffeln scolded and cursed; the more he scolded and cursed, the greater influence the unlucky star seemed to have, and the cattle became all the more stubborn. The other knights laughed and mocked and took great pleasure in the terrified floundering of the peasants and in von Stoffeln's anger. They had laughed at von Stoffeln's new castle built on the naked hilltop. Because of that he had vowed that there must be a beautiful avenue up there within a month's time. That was why he cursed and the knights laughed, while the peasants wept.

These last were seized by a terrible despair, for they no longer had a single cart that was not damaged, nor any team of cattle that was not harmed, nor had three beech trees been brought to the proper place within three days, and all strength had been exhausted.

Night had fallen, black clouds had gathered and there was lightning for the first time that year. The men had sat down by the roadside; it was the same turning of the road where they had sat three days earlier, but they did not realize this. There the Hornbach peasant, the husband of the woman from Lindau, was sitting with a couple of farm servants, and some others were also seated with them. They wanted to wait at that spot for beech trees that were supposed to be arriving from Sumiswald; they wanted to think over their misery undisturbed and to rest their bruised limbs.

Then a woman came along with a great basket on her head, moving so rapidly that there was almost a whistling, like the wind when it has been let loose out of closed spaces. It was Christine, the woman from Lindau whom the Hornbach peasant had taken on one occasion when he had gone on a warring expedition with his lord. She was not the sort of woman who is happy to be at home, to fulfil her duties in quietness and to care only for home and family. Christine wanted to know what was going on, and if she could not give her advice about something, it would turn out badly, or so she thought.

For this reason she had not sent a maid with the food, but had taken the heavy basket on her own head and had been looking for the men for a long time without success; she let fall bitter words on the subject as soon as she had found them. In the meantime, however, she had not been idle, for she could talk and work at the same time. She put down her basket, took the lid off the saucepan containing porridge, set out the bread and cheese in orderly fashion and placed the spoons in the porridge for her husband and his servants, and also told the others to tuck in as well, if they were still without food. Then she asked about the men's work, and how much had been accomplished in the two days. But the men had lost all appetite and all wish to talk; no one seized his spoon, and none had an answer. There was only one frivolous little farm servant fellow who didn't care whether there was rain or sunshine at harvest time, provided the year took its course and he had his wages and food on the table every mealtime; he seized his spoon and informed Christine that still no single beech tree had been planted and that everything was happening as if they had been bewitched.

Then the woman from Lindau mocked and scolded them, saying that this was nothing but vain imagining and that the men were behaving with the weakness of a woman in childbirth; they would bring no beech trees to Bärhegen, whether they toiled and wept or sat down and cried. It would be their own fault if the knight let them feel his wanton malice; but for the sake of the women and children the matter would have to be handled differently. Then a long black hand came suddenly over the woman's shoulder, and a piercing voice called, 'Yes, she's right!' And in their midst stood the green huntsman with his grinning face, and the red feather quivered on his hat. Immediately terror drove the men away from the spot; they scattered up the slope like chaff in a whirlwind.

Christine, the woman from Lindau, was the only one who could not flee; she was learning what it means to talk about the Devil and then be confronted by him in person. She stood as if transfixed by magic, compelled to stare at the red feather on his cap and to watch how the little red beard moved merrily up and down in the black face. The green huntsman gave a piercing laugh as the men disappeared, but he put on an amorous expression towards Christine and took her hand with a polite gesture. Christine wanted to withdraw it, but she could no longer escape the green huntsman; it seemed to her as if flesh were spluttering between red-hot tongs. And he began to speak fine words, and as he spoke his little red beard gleamed and moved lustfully up and down. He had not seen such a handsome little woman for a long time, he said, and it made his heart glad within his breast; what is more, he liked them bold, and in particular he liked those women best who could stay behind when the menfolk ran away. As he went on speaking in this way, the green huntsman appeared to Christine to become ever less terrifying. You could talk with a man like that, all the same, she thought, and she didn't see why she should run away; she had seen far uglier men than him before now. The thought came to her more and more that something could be done with a man like that, and if you knew how to talk to him in the right way, he would surely do you a favour, or in any case you could cheat him, just as you could cheat any other men. The green huntsman went on to say that he really did not know why people were so frightened by him, his intentions were so good towards everybody, and if people were so rude towards him, they mustn't be surprised if he did not always do to people what they most wanted. Then Christine took heart and told him that after all he did frighten people so much that it was terrible. Why had he demanded an unbaptized child? He surely could have spoken of other payment, one that would not seem so suspect to people, after all a child was a human being, and no Christian would go so far as to give away a child that was unbaptized. 'That is my payment, to which I am accustomed, and I shan't do the work for any other, and in any case why should any notice be taken of such a child that nobody as yet knows? It is when they are so young that you can give them away most easily, after all you have had neither pleasure nor trouble from them as yet. But the younger I can have them, the better, for the earlier I can bring up a child in my own way, the further I can mould it; but for that I don't need any christening, and won't have it either.' Then indeed Christine saw that he would content himself with no other reward, but the thought took root in her ever more firmly that this man was without doubt the one man who could not be deceived.

Therefore she said that if someone wanted to earn something he would have to content himself with the reward which could be given to him, but at the moment they had no unbaptized child in any of their houses, nor would there be one in a month's time, and the beech trees had to be delivered within this period. Then the green huntsman squirmed with politeness as he said, 'I am not demanding the child in advance. As soon as it is promised that the first child to be born will be handed over to me unbaptized, I shall be satisfied.' Christine was indeed very pleased at this. She knew that there would be no newborn child in the domain of her lords for some time to come. Now once the green huntsman had kept his promise and the beech trees were planted, it would not be necessary to give him anything in return, either a child or anything else; they would have masses read both as defence and offence, and would boldly scoff at the green huntsman, or so Christine thought. She therefore expressed her gratitude for the good offer and said this needed thinking over and she would like to speak to the menfolk about it. 'Yes,' said the green huntsman, 'but there is nothing more to think about or to talk over. I made an appointment with you for today, and now I want to know your answer; I've got a lot to do still at a good many places, and I don't exist simply on account of you people. You must accept or refuse; afterwards I don't want to hear anything more about the whole business.' Christine wanted to prevaricate about the matter, for she was reluctant to take it upon herself; indeed she would have liked to be coaxing, in order to be able to postpone the issue, but the green huntsman was in no humour for this and did not waver: 'Now or never!' he said. But as soon as the agreement about one single child was made, he would be willing to bring every night up onto Bärhegen as many beech trees as were delivered to him before midnight at the Kilchstalden down below; it was there that he would receive them. 'Now, pretty lady, don't hesitate!' the green huntsman said, and patted Christine on the cheek with irresistible charm. At that her heart did begin to beat hard, and she would have preferred to push the men forwards into this, so that she could have made out afterwards that it was their fault. But time pressed, there was no man there to be the scapegoat, and she clung to the belief that she was more cunning than the green huntsman and would have an idea that would enable her to get the better of him. So Christine said that she for her part was willing to agree, but if the menfolk later were unwilling, she could do nothing about that, and he was not to take it out of her. The green huntsman said that he would be well satisfied with her promise to do what she could. At this point, however, Christine did shudder, both with body and soul; now, she thought, would come the terrible moment when she would have to sign the agreement with the green huntsman in her own blood. But the green huntsman made it easier, saying that he never demanded signatures from pretty women and that he would be satisfied with a kiss. At this he pursed up his mouth towards Christine's face, and Christine could not escape; once more she was as if transfixed by magic, stiff and rigid. Then the pointed mouth touched Christine's face, and she felt as if some sharp-pointed steel fire were piercing marrow and bone, body and soul – and a yellow flash of lightning struck between them and showed Christine the green huntsman's devilish face gleefully distorted, and thunder rolled above them as if the heavens had split apart.

The green man had disappeared, and Christine stood as if petrified, as if her feet had become rooted deep down into the ground in that terrible moment. At last she regained the use of her limbs, but there was a whistling and roaring in her mind as if mighty waters were pouring their floods over towering high rocks down into a black abyss. Just as one does not hear one's own voice for the thundering of the waters, so Christine was not capable of knowing her own thoughts in the uproar that was thundering through her mind. Instinctively she fled up to the hill, and ever more fiercely did she feel a burning on her cheek where the green huntsman's mouth had touched her; she rubbed and washed, but the burning did not decrease.

The night became wild. Up in the air and in the ravines there was a fierce uproar as if the spirits of the night were holding a marriage feast in the black clouds and the winds were playing wild music for their horrible dances, as if the flashes of lightning were the wedding torches and the thunder the nuptial blessing. No one had ever previously experienced such a night at this time of year.

In the dark valley there was movement around one large house, and many people pressed around its sheltering roof. During a storm it usually happens that fear for his own hearth and home will drive the countryman under his own roof, where he can watch anxiously as long as the thunderstorm is in the sky above, guarding and protecting his own house. But now the common tribulation was greater than fear of the storm. The affliction brought them together in this house, which those whom the storm was driving from the Münneberg had to pass by as well as those who had taken flight from Bärhegen. Forgetting the terror of the night because of their own misery, they could be heard complaining and grumbling about their misfortune. In addition to all their misfortunes there had now come the violence of nature. Horses and oxen had become frightened and benumbed, had wrecked the carts, had hurled themselves over precipices, and many a creature groaned in deep pain from serious injuries, while others cried out loud as their shattered limbs were set and bound up.

Those who had seen the green huntsman also took flight in their terrible fear and joined in the misery of the others; here they told tremblingly of the repeated appearance of the figure. Trembling, the crowd listened to what the men told, pressed forwards from the wide, dark space nearer to the fire around which the men were seated, and when the wind blew through the rafters or the thunder rolled over the rooftop the crowd cried out and thought that the green huntsman was breaking through the roof to show himself in their midst. But when he did not come, when the terror of him subsided, when the old misery remained and the lamentations of the sufferers became louder, there gradually rose up those thoughts which are so prone to threaten a man's soul when he is in trouble. They began to calculate how much more worth they all were than one single unbaptized child; they increasingly forgot that guilt with regard to one soul weighs a thousand times more heavily than the rescuing of thousands upon thousands of human lives.

Gradually these thoughts made themselves heard and began to be mingled as comprehensible words into the groans of pain of the sufferers. People asked more closely about the green huntsman, grumbling that the others had not stood up to him better; he would not have taken anyone off, and the less you feared him, the less he would do to people. They might perhaps have been able to help the whole valley, if they had had their hearts in the right place. Then the men began to excuse themselves. They did not say that dealing with the Devil was no joke and that if you lent him an ear you would soon have to give him your whole head, but they spoke of the green huntsman's terrible appearance, his flaming beard, the fiery feather on his hat like a castle tower, and the terrible smell of sulphur which they had not cared to put up with. Christine's husband, however, who was used to his words becoming effective only after they had been confirmed by his wife, said that they should only ask his wife: she could tell them whether anybody could stand up to it; for everybody knew that she was a fearless woman. Then they all looked round for Christine, but nobody saw her. Each one had thought only of saving himself and no one else, and as each of them was now sitting where it was dry, he thought that all the others were too. Only now did it occur to them all that they had not seen Christine again since that terrible moment, and that she had not come into the house. Then her husband began to lament and all the others lamented with him, for it seemed to them all as if only Christine knew how to help. Suddenly the door opened, and Christine stood in their midst; her hair was dripping wet and her cheeks were red, while her eyes were burning more darkly than usual with a sinister fire. She was received with a sympathy to which she was not accustomed, and everybody wanted to tell her what had been thought and expressed and how much they had worried about her. Christine soon saw what this all meant and, hiding her inner fire behind mocking words, she reproached the men for their over-hasty flight and for the way none of them had taken any trouble about a poor woman and nobody had looked round to see what the green huntsman was up to with her. Then the storm of curiosity broke out, and everybody wanted first to know what the green huntsman had been doing with her, and those who were at the back stood up as high as they could in order to hear better and to see more closely the woman who had stood so near to the green huntsman. She wasn't to say anything, Christine said at first; they hadn't deserved it of her, they had treated her badly in the valley because she was a foreigner, the women had given her a bad name, the men had left her in the lurch everywhere, and if she had not been better intentioned than them all and if she had not had more courage than the lot of them, there would be no consolation nor way out for them at this very moment. Christine went on talking a long time in this way, reproaching the womenfolk harshly, who had never been willing to believe her that Lake Constance was bigger than the castle pond, and the more she was pressed, the more obstinate she seemed to become, and she insisted that people would put a wrong interpretation on what she had to say, and if all went well, would give her no thanks on that account; but if anything went wrong, it would be her fault and the entire responsibility would be placed upon her shoulders.

When finally the whole gathering was before Christine, begging and imploring her almost on their knees, and when those who were injured cried out loud and persisted in so doing, Christine seemed to relent and began to tell how she had stood firm and come to an agreement with the green huntsman – but she said nothing about the kiss, nor about the way it had burnt on her cheek and how her mind had been overwhelmed with the roaring noise. But she related what she had been considering since then in her downcast mind. The most important thing, she said, was that the beech trees would be taken up to Bärhegen; once they were up there, you could still see what could be done, and the main thing was that up till then as far as she knew no child would be born among them.

Many felt cold shivers down their spines at this account, but they were all pleased to think that they would still be able to see what could be done.

One young woman alone wept so bitterly that you could have washed your hands under her eyes, but she did not say anything. There was, however, one old woman, tall in appearance and with a presence that commanded respect, for her face was one which required obeisance or else compelled flight. She stepped into the middle of the room and said that to act like that would be to forget God, to risk losing what was certain for the sake of something uncertain, and to play with one's eternal salvation. Whoever had to do with the evil one would never escape from him, and whoever gave him a finger would lose body and soul to him. Nobody could help them from this distress but God, but whoever forsook God in time of trouble would himself be lost in time of trouble. But on this occasion the old woman's words were scorned and the young woman was told to be silent, for weeping and moaning would be no use here; another kind of help was needed now, they said.

It was soon agreed to try the arrangement. In the worst eventuality the business could hardly go badly; for it would not be the first time that men had deceived the most evil spirits, and if they themselves did not know what to do, a priest surely would give advice and find a way out. But in their darkness of mind many a one must have thought what he later admitted:

that he would not risk much money or time on account of an unbaptized child.

When the decision was taken according to Christine's wishes, it was as if all the whirlwinds were crashing together over the house top, as if armies of wild huntsmen were roaring overhead; the upright posts of the house quivered, the beams bent, trees splintered against the house like spears on a knight's breastplate. The people within turned pale and were overcome with horror, but they did not rescind their decision; when the grey light of dawn appeared they set about putting their counsel into effect.

The morning was beautiful and bright, thunder and lightning and witchcraft had vanished, the axes struck twice as sharply as before, the soil was friable and every beech tree fell straight, just as one would like it; none of the carts broke, the cattle were amenable and strong and the men were protected from all accidents as if by an invisible hand.

There was only one thing that was queer. At that time there was no track below Sumiswald leading to the lower valley; in that part there was still swampland which was watered by the uncontrollable river Grüne: one had to go up the slope and through the village past the church. As on the previous days they travelled always three teams together, so that they could help each other with advice, strength and cattle, and from that point onwards all they had to do was to go through Sumiswald, down the slope by the church on the other side of the village, and here there stood a little shrine; they had to lay out the beeches beyond the slope where the road was flat. As soon as they had come up the slope and were approaching the church on a level part of the road, the weight of the carts did not become lighter but heavier and heavier; they had to harness as many animals as they could muster, had to beat them unmercifully, had to lay hand on the spokes themselves to turn them, and what is more, even the quietest horses shied as if there were something invisible appearing from the churchyard that stood in their way, and a hollow sounding of a bell, almost like the misplaced noise of a distant death knell, came from the church, so that a peculiar sensation of horror seized even the strongest men, and every time that they approached the church, both men and beast shook with fear. Once they had passed beyond, they could move on quietly, unload quietly, and then go quietly back for a fresh load.

On that same day the peasants unloaded six beech trees and placed them side by side at the agreed spot; the next morning six beech trees had been planted up on Bärhegen and throughout the whole valley nobody had heard an axle turning over on its hub, and nobody had heard the usual calling of carters, the neighing of horses or the monotonous bellowing of oxen. But there were six beech trees standing up there, anybody could see them who wanted to, and they were the six trees which had been laid down at the foot of the slope, and no other ones.

At that there was great astonishment throughout the valley, and many people's curiosity was aroused. The knights especially wondered what kind of agreement the peasants had made and by what means the beech trees had been transported to the spot. They would have gladly used heathenish means of forcing the secret from the peasants. However, they soon realized that the peasants too did not know all and were themselves half terrified. Furthermore, von Stoffeln resisted them. He was not only indifferent about how the trees came to Bärhegen, but, on the contrary, he was glad that the peasants were not being exhausted in the process, provided only that the trees did arrive there. He had indeed realized that the mockery of his knights had misled him to a foolish action, for if the peasants were ruined and the fields not cultivated it was the ruling class which would suffer the greater loss; but once von Stoffeln had given an order, it had to stand. Therefore the relief which the peasants had obtained for themselves suited him quite well, and he was wholly indifferent whether in consequence they had forsworn their souls' salvation – for what did he care about the souls of peasants, once death had taken their bodies. Now he laughed at his knights and protected the peasants from their wantonness. In spite of this the knights wanted to get to the bottom of the business and sent squires to keep watch; these were found the next morning lying half dead in ditches, hurled there by an invisible hand.

Then two knights set off to Bärhegen. They were bold warriors, and where there had been any hazardous enterprise to be faced in heathen lands, they had faced it. They were found the next morning lying unconscious on the ground, and when they recovered their speech they said that they had been hurled down by a red knight with a fiery lance. Here and there could be found an inquisitive woman who could not refrain from looking out at midnight from a crack in the timber or from a dormer window to the road in the valley. Immediately a poisonous wind blew up at such a one, so that the face swelled up, and for weeks afterwards nose and eyes could not be seen and her mouth could be found only with difficulty. That made people less anxious to indulge in peeping, and no single eye looked out when midnight lay over the valley.

On one occasion, however, death came suddenly upon a man; he needed the last sacraments, but nobody could fetch the priest, since it was almost midnight, and the way lay past the Kilchstalden. So an innocent little boy, dear in the sight of God and man, ran to Sumiswald without informing anybody, impelled by anxiety for his father. When he came to the Kilchstalden he saw beech trees rising up from the ground, each one drawn by two fiery squirrels, and nearby he saw a green huntsman riding on a black ram, with a fiery whip in his hand, a fiery beard on his face and a feather swaying red hot on his hat. The transport flew high into the air over all the slopes and as quick as a flash. This is what the lad saw, and no harm came to him.

Before three weeks had passed, ninety beech trees were standing on Bärhegen, making a beautiful shaded walk, for all the trees put out shoots luxuriantly and none of them withered. But neither the knights nor von Stoffeln himself went walking there often, for every time they were seized by a secret horror; they would rather have known nothing further about the business, but nobody made a suggestion that the work should be stopped, and each comforted himself by saying that if things went wrong it would be somebody else's fault.

But the peasants felt easier with every beech tree that was planted up on top, for with every tree grew the hope that their lord would be satisfied and the green huntsman deceived; after all, he had no guarantee, and once the hundredth tree was up there, what did they care about the green huntsman? Nevertheless they were still not certain about the matter; every day they were afraid that he might play them a trick and leave them in the lurch. On 25th May, St Urban's day, they brought him the last beeches to the Kilchstalden, and neither old nor young slept much that night; it was scarcely believable that he would complete the work without making some trouble, if he were without a child or any surety.

The next morning old and young were up long before sunrise, for everyone was impelled by the same inquisitive anxiety, but it was a long time before anybody ventured to the place where the beech trees had been put: perhaps there would be some trap there for those who wished to deceive the green huntsman.

A wild cowherd who had brought goats down from high mountain pasture finally dared to go forwards; he found no beech trees lying on the ground, nor could any trace of trickery be perceived at that spot. They still had no trust in the business; the cowherd had to go ahead of them to Bärhegen. There everything was in order, a hundred beech trees stood in full array, none was withered, nobody's face swelled up, nobody had pains in any limb. Then their hearts became exultant, and much mockery could be heard at the expense of the green huntsman and the knights. For the third time they sent out the wild cowherd and had him inform von Stoffeln that everything was now in order on Bärhegen, and that he might like to come and count the beech trees. But von Stoffeln felt terrified, and he sent them the message that they should see to it that they went home. He would have gladly told them to remove the whole avenue of trees, but he did not do this on account of his knights; he did not know about the peasants' compact and who it was who might intervene in the business.

When the cowherd brought the message, hearts swelled yet more with defiance; wild youths danced in the avenue, a wild yodelling resounded from ravine to ravine, from one mountain to another, and re-echoed from the walls of Sumiswald castle. Thoughtful older people admonished and pleaded, but defiant hearts do not pay attention to the warnings of cautious old age, and then once the misfortune has come about, the old people are blamed for it on account of their hesitation and warnings. The time has not yet come when it is recognized that when defiance stamps its foot, misfortune grows forth from the ground. The rejoicing spread over hill and vale into all the houses, and wherever a finger's length of smoked meat remained, it was taken down and prepared for eating, and wherever a lump of butter as big as a hand remained in a basin, it was used for baking.

The meat was eaten, the fritters disappeared, day had gone and a new day rose in the sky. Nearer and nearer came the day when a woman should bear a child; and the nearer the day, the more urgently did the fear become renewed that the green huntsman would announce himself again and demand what was his by right, or else prepare a trap for them.

Who could measure the distress of that young woman who was to give birth to the child? Her cries of despair resounded throughout the whole house, gradually affecting all who lived there, and nobody could give any counsel, apart from saying that there was no trusting that huntsman whom they had had the dealings with. The nearer the fateful hour came, the more closely the poor woman pressed to God, embraced the Holy Mother not with her arms alone but with body and soul and whole mind, praying for protection for the sake of her blessed son. And it became clearer and clearer to her that in life and death in every need the greatest comfort is in God, for where He is, the evil one may not be and has no power.

Her soul was convinced ever more clearly that if a priest of the Lord were present at the birth with that holiest of all things, the sacred body of the Redeemer, and if he were armed with strong sentences of anathema, no evil spirit would dare to draw near, and at once the priest would be able to provide the newborn child with the sacrament of baptism, as was allowed by custom at that time; then the poor child would be removed for ever from the danger which the presumption of its fathers had brought upon it. This belief came to be shared by others, and the young woman's wretched plight went to their hearts, but they fought shy of confessing to the priest their pact with Satan, and since that time nobody had gone to confession nor had given an account of themselves to him. The priest was a very pious man, and even the knights of the castle did not make fun of him, though he told them the truth straight. What the peasants had thought was that once the business was over he could do nothing to stop them, but all the same nobody now wanted to be the first to tell him, and their consciences told them why.

At last the wretchedness of the situation moved one woman to take action; she went off and disclosed to the priest the compact and what it was the poor woman wanted. The pious man was greatly shocked, but he did not waste time with empty words; he boldly took up the fight with the mighty enemy on behalf of a poor soul. He was one of those men who do not fear the hardest fight, because they wish to be crowned with the crown of eternal life, and because indeed they know that no man will be crowned unless he fights well.

He drew a consecrated circle with holy water about the house where the woman was awaiting her time, for no evil spirits might step into this circle; he blessed the threshold and the whole room, and the woman had a quiet labour and the priest baptized the child without any disturbance. Outside all was quiet, bright stars sparkled in the clear sky and gentle breezes played in the trees. Some people said they heard laughter like a horse's neighing from afar, but others thought it was only the owls at the edge of the wood.

Everyone present, however, was highly delighted, and all fear had disappeared – for ever, as they thought; for if they had fooled the green huntsman once, they could go on doing so by the same method.

A great feast was prepared, and guests were invited from far and wide. The priest of the Lord warned them in vain against feasting and rejoicing, told them to be fearful and to pray, for the enemy was not yet overcome nor God propitiated. He felt in his mind that he was not in a position to lay any act of penance upon them, and that a mighty and heavy punishment was approaching from God's own hand. But they did not listen to him and wanted to satisfy him with invitations to food and drink. He, however, went sadly away, prayed for those who did not know what they were doing, and armed himself with prayer and fasting to fight like a true shepherd for the flock entrusted to his care.

Christine too was sitting in the midst of the jubilant throng, but she sat strangely still with glowing cheeks and sombre eyes, and one could see a strange twitching in her face. Christine, as an experienced midwife, had been present at the birth, and had acted as godmother during the hasty christening ceremony with an insolent, fearless heart, but when the priest sprinkled the water over the child and baptized it in the three holy names, she felt as if someone were suddenly pressing a red-hot iron on the spot where she had received the green huntsman's kiss. She had started in sudden terror, had almost dropped the child onto the ground, and since that time the pain had not decreased but burned more from hour to hour. At first she had sat still, had forced back the pain and kept to herself the dark thoughts which were turning in her awakened mind, but she moved her hand ever more frequently to the burning spot, on which a poisonous wasp seemed to be placed, piercing with a burning sting right into her marrow. But as there was no wasp to be chased away and as the stings became ever more burning and her thoughts ever more dreadful, Christine began to show people her cheek and ask them what could be seen on it, and she kept on asking, but nobody saw anything, and soon nobody had any wish to be diverted from the pleasures of the christening celebration by peering at her cheeks. Finally she found an old woman who was willing to look carefully; just at that moment the cock crowed, the grey of dawn came, so that what the old woman saw on Christine's cheek was an almost invisible spot. It was nothing, she said, it would go away all right, and she moved off.

And Christine tried to comfort herself that it was nothing and it would go away soon; but the pain did not lessen, and the little spot grew imperceptibly, and everybody saw it and asked her what that black thing was on her face. They did not mean anything special by it, but their remarks went to her heart like sword thrusts, rekindled her dark thoughts, and she could not avoid coming back to the thought, time and time again, that it was on this very spot that the green huntsman had kissed her, and that the same fire which on that occasion had shot through her limbs like lightning, now remained burning and consuming there. Thus she could not sleep, her food tasted like firebrand, she rushed aimlessly about, seeking consolation but finding none, for the pain increased still further, and the black spot became bigger and blacker, single dark streaks ran out from the spot, and down towards the mouth it seemed as if there was a lump planted on the round spot.

In this way Christine suffered and rushed around many a long day and many a long night without revealing to anyone the fear in her heart and what it was she had received from the green huntsman on this spot; but if she had known how she could have got rid of this pain, she would have given anything in heaven or on earth to do it. She was by nature a brazen woman, but now she had gone wild with angry pain.

It now happened that once again a woman was expecting a child. This time there was no great fear and people were easy in mind; so long as they saw to the priest coming at the right time, they thought they could defy the green huntsman. It was only Christine who did not share this belief. The nearer the day of the birth came, the more terrible the burning on her cheek became, the more violently the black spot extended, stretching out legs visibly, driving up short hairs, while shining points and strips appeared on its back and the hump became a head out of which there blazed a poisonous brilliance as if from two eyes. Everyone who saw the poisonous spider on Christine's cheek shrieked aloud, and they fled full of fear and horror when they saw how this spider sat firm on her face and had grown out from her flesh. People said all kinds of things, some advised this, some advised the other, but all wished Christine joy of it, whatever it was, and all avoided her and fled from her whenever this was possible. The more people fled from her, the more Christine was driven to follow them, and she rushed from house to house; she must have felt that the Devil was reminding her of the promised child, and she rushed after folk in hellish fear to persuade them in no uncertain words to make the sacrifice required by the pact. But the others were little troubled by this; what was tormenting Christine did not hurt them, and what she was suffering was in their opinion her own responsibility, and if they could no longer escape from her, they said to her: 'That's your affair! Nobody has promised a child, and therefore nobody is going to give one.' She set about her own husband with furious words. He fled like the rest, and when he could no longer avoid her he cold-bloodedly told her that it would get better all right, it was a spot such as many people had; once it had taken its course, the pain would cease, and it would be easy to disperse it.

Meanwhile, however, the pain did not cease, each leg was hellfire, the spider's body hell itself, and when the woman's appointed time came, Christine felt as if a sea of fire were surging around her, as if fiery knives were boring into her marrow, as if fiery whirlwinds were rushing through her brain. But the spider swelled and arched itself up, and its eyes glared viciously from between the short bristles. When Christine found no sympathy anywhere in her burning agony and saw that the woman in labour was strongly guarded, she burst forth like a madwoman along the road where the priest would have to come.

The latter was coming up the slope at a quick pace, accompanied by the sturdy sexton; the hot sun and the steep road did not slow down their walk, for it was a matter of saving a soul and of preventing an eternal misfortune; coming from a visit to a sick parishioner who lived a long way off, the priest was anxious on account of the fearful delay he had experienced. In desperation, Christine threw herself before him in the road, clasped his knees, begged for release from her hell, for the sacrifice of the child that was not yet born, and the spider swelled still more, gleamed terrible and black in Christine's red swollen face, and with terrifying glances it glared at the priest's holy requisites. But the priest pushed Christine quickly to one side and made the holy sign; he saw the enemy well enough, but desisted from the fight in order to save a soul. But Christine started up, stormed after him and did her utmost to stop him; yet the sexton's strong hand held the woman off from the priest, and the latter could just arrive in time to protect the house, to receive the infant into his consecrated hands and to place it into the hands of Him Whom hell never overcomes.

Meanwhile Christine had been undergoing a terrible struggle outside. She wanted to have the unbaptized child in her hands and wanted to force her way into the house, but strong men prevented her. Gusts of wind buffeted against the house and yellow lightning hissed round it, but the hand of the Lord was above it, the child was baptized, and Christine circled round the house in vain and without power. Seized by ever wilder hellish torture, she emitted sounds which did not resemble sounds that might come from a human breast; the cattle quivered in their sheds and tore loose from their halters, while the tops of the oak trees in the forest rustled in terror.

Inside the house there was rejoicing over the new victory, the impotence of the green huntsman, the vain writhings of his accessory, but Christine lay outside, thrown onto the ground by dreadful pains, and her face was seized by labour pains such as no woman in childbirth has ever experienced on this earth, and the spider in her face swelled higher and higher and burned ever more searingly through her limbs.

Then Christine felt as if her face were bursting open, as if burning coals were being born, coming to life and crawling away over her face, over all her limbs, as if her whole face were coming to life and crawling away red-hot over all her body. In the pale light from the lightning she now saw black little spiders, long-legged, poisonous and innumerable, running over her limbs out into the night, and after those that had disappeared there ran others, long-legged, poisonous and innumerable. Finally she could see no more following the earlier ones, the fire in her face subsided, the spider settled down, became once more an almost invisible point and looked with weary eyes out at the hellish brood which it had borne and sent forth, as a sign that the green huntsman would not let himself be made a fool of.

Exhausted like a woman who has just given birth to a child, Christine crept into the house; although the fire no longer burned so hot on her face, the fire in her heart had not abated, even if her weary limbs longed for rest, for the green huntsman would give her no more rest: once he has got somebody, that is how he treats them.

Inside the house, however, there was jubilation and rejoicing, and for a long time they did not hear how the cattle were bellowing and raging in the cowshed. At last they did start up, and a few went out to see; when those who had gone out returned they came back pale as death with the news that the best cow lay dead and the rest of them were raging and stampeding in such a way as had never been seen before. It wasn't right, there was something unusual at the back of it, they said. At that the sounds of rejoicing were silenced and everyone ran out to the cattle, whose bellowing could be heard over hill and valley, but nobody had any suggestions. They tried both worldly and spiritual arts against magic, but all in vain; already before day broke, death had laid low all the cattle in the shed. But when it became silent in one farm, the bellowing started up on another farm, and yet another; those who were there heard how the trouble had broken into their cattle sheds and how the animals called to their masters for help in their terrible fear.

They rushed home as if flames were leaping from their rooftops, but there was nothing they could do; on one farm as on another death laid low the cattle; cries of distress from man and beast filled hills and valleys, and the sun which had set leaving the valley so happy rose to gaze upon scenes of awful distress. When the sun shone, people at last could see how the sheds where the cattle had been stricken were teeming with countless black spiders. These creatures crawled over the cattle, and the cattle food which they touched became poisoned, and any living creature began to rage until soon it was felled by death. It was impossible to get rid of these spiders from any cattle shed where they had penetrated, it was as if they grew out of the ground itself; it was impossible to protect any shed where they had not yet entered from their invasion, for unexpectedly they started creeping out of all the walls and would fall in clusters from the threshing floor. The cattle were then driven out to pasture, but it was simply driving them into death's jaws. For wherever a cow placed her foot onto grassland, the ground began to come to life: black, long-legged spiders sprouted up, horrible Alpine flowers which crawled onto the cattle, and a fearful wailing could be heard from the hilltops down to the valley. And all these spiders resembled the spider on Christine's face as children resemble their mother, and nobody had ever seen such before.

The noise of the wretched animals had penetrated to the castle too, and soon shepherds followed with the news that their cattle had fallen because of the poisonous animals, and von Stoffeln heard with ever increasing anger how herd upon herd had been lost; now he learnt what type of pact his peasants had made with the green huntsman, and how the huntsman had been deceived a second time, and how the spiders resembled, as children their mother, the spider on the face of the woman from Lindau who alone had made the compact with the green huntsman and had never given a proper account of what had happened. Then von Stoffeln rode up the hill in fierce anger and roared at the peasants that he was not going to lose herd upon herd for their sake; they would have to keep any promises that they had made; what they had done of their own free will, they would have to put up with. He wasn't going to suffer damage on their account, or if he did have to suffer, they would have to make it good to him a thousand times over. They would have to look out. In this way he spoke to them, indifferent to what it was he was expecting of them; it did not occur to him that he had driven them to it, for he only took account of what they had done.

It had already dawned upon most of the peasants that the spiders were a visitation of the evil one, a warning that they should keep the agreement; that Christine must know more about it, and that she had not told them all about her agreement with the green huntsman. Now they all trembled again at the thought of the green huntsman and no longer laughed at him, and they trembled before their temporal lord; if they did placate their overlords, what would their spiritual lord say about it, would he allow this, and would he not then lay any penance upon them? The leading peasants met in their fear in a solitary shed, and Christine was to come there and give a clear account of what exactly she had agreed with the green huntsman.

Christine came, more savage, thirsting for revenge, again racked by the growing spider.

When she saw the hesitation of the men and realized that there were no women there, she related exactly what had happened to her: how the green huntsman had quickly taken her at her word and had given her a kiss as a token to which she had not paid any attention any more than to other kisses; how the spider had now grown in hellish pain on that same spot from the moment onwards when the first child had been baptized; how the spider had given birth in hellish agonies to an innumerable host of spiders as soon as the second child had been born and the green huntsman had been fooled; for it was obvious that you could not fool him and get away with it, as she herself felt in her thousandfold pains of death. Now the spider was growing again, she said, the pain was increasing, and if the next child were not given to the green huntsman, nobody could tell how horrible a calamity might break out upon them, and how horrible the knight's vengeance might be.

This is what Christine said, and the men's hearts throbbed, and for a long time nobody was willing to speak. Gradually broken sounds pressed forth from their frightened throats, and when these sounds were pieced together, it was evident that the peasants thought exactly as Christine did, but they insisted that not one of them had given his consent to her action. One of the men stood up and said shortly and sharply that it seemed to him that the best thing was to kill Christine, for once she was dead, the green huntsman could do as he pleased with her, but would have no further claim on the living. Then Christine laughed wildly, stepped close up to him and said into his face that he could hit out at her, it was all the same to her, but the green huntsman wasn't interested in her, but in an unbaptized child, and just as he had laid his mark on her, so he could mark the hand which wrongfully seized her. Then there was a twitching in the hand of this one man who had spoken, he sat down and silently listened to the advice of the others. In tentative, fragmentary phrases, of the type where nobody says everything but each speaker only says something that is intended to mean little, an agreement was made that the next child should be sacrificed; but nobody was willing to lend a hand here by carrying the child to the Kilchstalden where the beech trees had been laid out. Nobody had been reluctant to use the Devil for what they considered to be the general good, but nobody wanted to meet him personally. Then Christine offered herself willingly for this, for if one has had to do with the Devil on one occasion, it could do little further harm a second time. It was known who was to give birth to the next child, but nothing was said about it, and the father of the child was not present. After making this agreement, which was both a spoken and an unspoken one, they dispersed.

The young woman who had trembled and wept without knowing why on that dreadful night when Christine had given her account of the green huntsman was now expecting the next child. What had happened in the previous cases did not make her feel cheerful and confident, an indefinable fear lay upon her heart which she could not remove either by prayer or confession. It seemed to her as if she were encircled by a conspiracy of silence, nobody spoke about the spider any more, all eyes which looked at her seemed to her suspicious, and seemed to be calculating the hour when they might seize upon her child in order to placate the Devil.

She felt so lonely and forlorn in face of the secret power around her; the only support she had was her mother-in-law, a pious woman who remained faithful to her, but what can an old woman do against a wild crowd? She had her husband who had indeed promised all good things, but how he wailed about his cattle and how little he thought of his poor wife's anxiety! The priest had promised to come as quickly and as soon as they might ask, but what could happen during the period after he had been sent for and before he arrived? And the poor woman had no reliable messenger except her husband, who should be her protection and guard, and, what is more, the poor woman lived in one house with Christine, and their husbands were brothers, and she had no relations of her own, for she had come into the house as an orphan! You can imagine the poor woman's anxiety of heart; she could find some confidence only when she prayed with her good mother-in-law, but this confidence at once disappeared again as soon as she saw the evil looks around her.

Meanwhile the sickness was still there, keeping the terror alive. It was true that it was only here or there that one of the animals died, if the spiders showed themselves. But as soon as the terror lessened at one farm or as soon as somebody said, or thought, that the bad business was becoming less serious of its own accord and that one should think twice before treating a child sinfully, Christine's hellish pains flamed up, the spider swelled high and the man who had thought or talked in this way discovered that death had returned among his herd of cattle with renewed rage. Yes, the nearer the expected hour came, the more the distress seemed to increase again, and people realized that they would have to make a definite arrangement about how they were to get hold of the child safely and without fail. They were most afraid of the husband, and they were loath to use violence against him. He said he did not want to know about the business; he was willing to do as his wife asked and fetch the priest, but he agreed not to hurry about it, and what might happen in his absence was not his business. In this way he placated his conscience; he would placate God through extra masses, and it might still be possible to do something for the poor child's soul, he thought; perhaps the pious priest would wrest the child back from the Devil, and then he and the other peasants would be out of the business; they would have done their part and at the same time still cheated the evil one. That is what the husband thought, and in any case, however matters turned, he argued, he himself would have no responsibility for the whole business, since he was not taking any active part with his own hands.

In this manner the poor wife had been sold and did not know it; she anxiously went on hoping that rescue would come; the stab to her heart had been decided in the counsel of the people – but what He above had decreed was still covered by the clouds which hide the future.

It was a year of storms, and harvest time had come; all possible strength was being mobilized, in order to bring the grain safely under cover during the bright periods. A hot afternoon had come, the clouds stretched their black heads over the dark peaks, the swallows fluttered fearfully around the roof, and the poor wife felt so constrained and anxious alone in the house, for even the grandmother was outside in the fields, helping more with good intentions than with deeds. Then the pain pierced double-edged through the woman's marrow and bones, everything went dark in front of her eyes, she felt her hour approaching and was alone. Fear drove her out of the house, with dragging feet she walked out to the field, but soon had to sit down; she wanted to call out into the distance, but her voice would not leave her heavily breathing breast. There was with her a little lad who had only just learnt how to walk and who had never gone to the field on his own legs but only in his mother's arms. The poor woman had to use this boy as her messenger; she did not know whether he would be able to find the field or whether his little legs could carry him there. But the faithful lad saw how anxious his mother was, and ran, and fell down, and stood up again, and the cat chased his pet rabbit, doves and hens ran about his feet, his pet lamb jumped after him, playfully pushing; but the boy saw nothing of it, did not let himself be held up and faithfully delivered his message.

The grandmother appeared in breathless haste, but the husband delayed; he only wanted to finish stacking up the cartload, was the message. An eternity passed, at last he came, and another eternity passed, at last he set out on the long road, and the poor wife felt in deathly fear how her time was drawing more and more quickly upon her.

Christine had been gleefully watching everything outside in the field. The sun might burn hot as she worked at the heavy labour, but the spider hardly burned any more at all, and for the next few hours walking seemed easy to her. She got on with the work happily and was in no hurry to return home, for she knew how slow the messenger was going to be. It was not until the last sheaf had been loaded and gusts of wind announced the approaching storm that she made haste towards her prey which she thought was so safely hers. And as she walked home, she waved knowingly to various passers-by, and they nodded to her and quickly took the news to their own homes; there was much sinking at the knees where the news was heard, and many souls wanted to pray in their involuntary fear, but could not do so.

Inside the little room the poor woman was whimpering, and each minute became an eternity, and the grandmother could not allay the extreme distress, even though she prayed and spoke consolingly. She had locked up the room carefully and placed heavy furniture in front of the door. As long as they were alone in the house, it was still tolerable, but when they saw Christine coming home, when they heard her slinking step by the door, when they heard many another footstep outside and secret whispering, and no priest nor any faithful person showed himself, and when the moment, usually longed for so intensely, approached nearer and nearer, you can imagine how the poor women in their fear were as if swimming in boiling oil, without help and without hope. They heard how Christine would not move from the door; the poor woman could feel the fiery eyes of her wild sister-in-law piercing through the door and burning her through body and soul. Then the first whimpering sign of new life was heard through the door, stifled as quickly as possible, but too late. The door flew open from a violent lurch which Christine had been waiting to give all this time, and just as a tiger leaps upon its prey, so Christine leaps upon the poor woman in childbirth. The old woman who throws herself to meet the storm is hurled down; the woman in childbirth pulls herself together in a mother's holy fear, but her weak body collapses, and the child is in Christine's hands; a ghastly cry bursts from the mother's heart, and then she is enshrouded in the black shadows of unconsciousness.

Hesitation and horror seized the men as Christine came out with the stolen child. The anticipation of a terrible future was revealed to them, but nobody had the courage to stop the deed, and fear of the Devil's visitations was stronger than the fear of God. Christine alone did not hesitate; her face gleamed burning, like that of a victorious warrior after the fight, and it seemed to her as if the spider were caressing her with a soft tickling; the flashes of lightning which had licked around her on her way to the Kilchstalden now seemed to be cheerful lights, while the thunder sounded like a gentle growl, and the vengeful storm like a pleasant rustling.

Hans, the poor woman's wretched husband, had kept his word only too well. He had made his way slowly, had looked ponderingly at every field, watched every bird and waited to see how the fish in the stream leapt up to catch flies just before the storm broke. Then he started forwards with rapid steps and prepared to take a jump; there was something within him which drove him to it and made his hair stand on end: it was his conscience, which told him what a father deserved if he betrayed his wife and child; it was the love which he still bore to his wife and to his own seed. But then there was something else which held him back, and that was stronger than the first thing: it was fear of other people, fear of the Devil and love of those things which the Devil could take from him. Then he went more slowly again, slowly as a man who is taking his last walk, the walk to the scaffold. Perhaps this really was the case, for after all many a man does not know that the walk he is taking may be his last; if he did not know this, he would not set out on it, or else he would do so in another spirit.

Thus it was late before he came to Sumiswald. Black clouds raced across over the Münneberg, heavy drops of rain fell, hissing in the hot dust, and the little bell in the church tower began its hollow ringing to admonish the people to think of God and to beg that His storm should not become a judgement upon them. The priest stood in front of his house, prepared for any journey to his parishioners, and ready to set out to a dying man, to a burning house or whatever else it might be, if his Master, Who was moving above him across the heavens, should call upon him. When he saw Hans coming he recognized that this was a call to a difficult task; he wrapped his robes firmly about him and sent word to his sexton that he should find someone else to take his place as bell-ringer. In the meantime he provided Hans with a cool drink which would be so refreshing after the quick walk in the sultry atmosphere, though Hans had no need of it; but the priest did not suspect the man's deceitfulness. Hans took his refreshment slowly and deliberately. The sexton appeared, but in no hurry, and gladly shared in the drink which Hans offered him. The priest stood accoutred before them, scorning any drink which he did not need for the walk and the struggle ahead. He did not like to tell anyone to leave the drink he had before him and to infringe a guest's privileges, but he knew a law which was higher than the law of hospitality, and this leisurely drinking made him impatient with anger.

At last he told them that he was ready, that a distressed woman was waiting and that an appalling misdeed was threatening them; he would have to come between the woman and the evil deed with his holy weapons, and therefore they were to come without further delay; up above there would still be something for the man who had not quenched his thirst here below. Then Hans, the husband of the woman who was waiting, replied that there was no particular hurry, as his wife was slow and had difficulties about everything. And at once a flash of lightning burst into the room so that they were all blinded by it, and a clap of thunder sounded over the house so that every post and beam trembled. Then after he had finished his prayer of blessing the sexton said: 'Hark at the weather outside; the heavens themselves have confirmed what Hans said, that we ought to wait, and what use would it be if we did go, we should never get there alive, and after all he said himself that there would be no need to hurry in the case of his wife.'

And truly the storm was pelting down in a way that is seldom seen more than once in a lifetime. It was raging from every cleft and valley, from all sides, and from all quarters the winds were driving in upon Sumiswald, and every cloud became an army of warriors, and one cloud stormed upon another, one cloud wanted the other cloud's life, and a battle of the clouds began, and the storm stood its ground, and flash after flash of lightning was let loose, and flash after flash was slung down to earth as if the lightning were trying to cut a passage down through the centre of the earth and out onto the other side. The thunder roared without intermission, the storm howled angrily, the clouds' belly burst open, and floods poured down. When the battle of the clouds broke out so suddenly and violently, the priest had not answered the sexton, but neither had he sat down; an ever mounting anxiety seized hold of him, and an urge came upon him to plunge out into the raging of the elements, though he hesitated on account of his companions. Then he seemed to hear above the terrible voice of the thunder the piercing cry of a woman in labour. Then the thunder appeared to him all at once as God's terrible reproach for his delay; he prepared to set out, whatever the other two might say. Ready for whatever might come, he stepped out into the fiery raging of the tempest and the downpour from the clouds; the two others followed slowly and reluctantly behind him.

There was a roaring and whistling and raging, as if these sounds were to fuse into the last trump heralding the end of the world, and sheaves of fire fell upon the village, as if every house were to burst into flames, but the servant of Him Who gives His voice to the thunder and uses the lightning as His servant need have no fear of this fellow servant of the same Lord, and whoever goes on God's errands can confidently leave God's weather to take care of itself. Hence the priest walked fearlessly through the storm to the Kilchstalden, carrying with him the hallowed holy weapons, and his heart was with God. But the others did not follow him with the same courage, for their hearts were not in the same place; they did not wish to go down the Kilchstalden, not in such weather and at such an hour, and, what is more, Hans had a special reason to be reluctant. They begged the priest to turn back, to go another way: Hans knew a nearer path, while the sexton knew a better one, and both warned him against the floods in the valley from the swollen river Grüne. But the priest did not hear and took no notice of what they said; urged on by an unaccountable impulse, he hastened towards the Kilchstalden on the wings of prayer, no stone catching his feet and no lightning blinding his eyes; Hans and the sexton followed behind trembling, and protected, as they thought, by the holy sacraments which the priest himself was carrying.

But when they arrived in view of the village, where the slope goes down to the valley below, the priest suddenly halts and puts his hand over his eyes for protection. Beyond the shrine a red feather gleams in the light of the lightning, and the priest's sharp eye sees a black head rearing up from the green hedgerow, and on the head the red feather. And as he goes on looking, he sees a wild figure coming down the opposite slope in rapid flight, as if driven by the wind's wild fury, hastening towards the dark head upon which the red feather was swaying like a flag.

At that the priest was enflamed by the sacred fighting urge which comes upon those whose hearts are dedicated to God as soon as they sense the imminence of the evil one; it comes like the growth of life upon the seed of corn or the opening flower or upon the warrior who is confronted by his opponent's drawn sword. And the priest rushed down the slope like a thirsting man towards the cool waters of a river or a hero into battle, rushed into fiercest battle, thrust himself between the green huntsman and Christine as she was about to place the child in the evil one's arms, and hurled the three holy names into their midst; he holds up the holy implement before the green huntsman's face, dashes holy water over the child and at the same time catches Christine with it. Thereupon the green huntsman makes off with a terrifying howl of pain, flashing by like a red-hot strip until the earth swallows him up; after being touched by the holy water Christine shrivels up with a frightful hissing, like wool in fire or quicklime in water, shrivels up, hissing and flame-spraying, until nothing remains but the black, swollen, ghastly spider in her own face, shrivels into it, hisses into it, and now this spider sits distended with poison and defiant, right on the child, and shoots angry flashes of lightning from her eyes at the priest. The latter throws holy water at her, which hisses like ordinary water on a hot stone; the spider grows bigger and bigger, and extends her black legs further and further over the child, glaring ever more poisonously at the priest; with the courage of his burning faith the priest now stretches out a daring hand towards her. It is as if he were plunging his hand into red-hot thorns, but he holds fast undeterred, hurls the verminous creature away, picks up the child and takes it to the mother without further delay.

And as the priest's struggle ended, the battle of the clouds abated too, and they hurried off to their dark chambers; soon the valley in which the fiercest battle had just been raging was shimmering in the quiet light of the stars, and almost breathlessly the priest reached the house where the crime had been committed against mother and child.

The mother was still lying in a faint, for she had lost consciousness after emitting her piercing cry; the old woman sat praying by her side, for she still trusted God and believed His strength was greater than the Devil's wickedness. By returning the child the priest also restored life to the mother. When she saw her baby again as she awoke, she was permeated by a rapture such as is only known to the angels in heaven, and the priest baptized the child as it lay in its mother's arms in the name of God the Father, Son and Holy Spirit – and now the infant was snatched from the Devil's power for ever, unless it should at some future time submit of its own accord to the evil one. But God protected the infant from this fate; the newborn soul was given into God's care, while the body lay poisoned by the spider.

Soon the soul departed from this life, and the little body was marked as if by burns. The poor mother wept indeed, but when each part returns to where it belongs, the soul to God, the body to the earth, consolation will come, more quickly to one person perhaps, and more slowly to another.

As soon as the priest had fulfilled his holy office, he began to feel a strange itching in the hand and arm with which he had hurled away the spider. He noticed small, black blotches on his hand which grew visibly larger and swelled up; the shudder of death penetrated to his heart. He gave the two women his blessing and hurried home, wishing, faithful warrior that he was, to bring back the holy weapons to the place where they belonged, so that they might be at hand for his successor. His arm became distended, and black boils swelled up more and more fiercely; he was fighting against the exhaustion of death, but did not succumb to it.

When he came to the Kilchstalden he saw Hans, the godless father whose whereabouts had been known to nobody, lying on his back in the middle of the road. His face was terribly swollen and black with burns, and there sitting right on top of him was the spider, big, black and gruesome. When the priest came, it puffed itself up, its hairs stood poisonously on end on its back, its eyes glared fiercely at him, and it was behaving like a cat which is preparing to spring at the face of a deadly enemy. Then the priest began to say a prayer and lifted up the holy implements, so that the spider cringed in terror and slunk on its long legs away from the black face until it was concealed in the hissing grass. After that the priest went on home, where he put the holy implements in their proper place, and, while fierce pains were racking his body to death, his soul waited in sweet contentment for God, on Whose account it had been so valiantly fighting the good fight – and God did not let the soul wait long.

But such sweet peace which waits patiently on the will of the Lord was not to be found down in the valley or up on the hills.

From the moment when Christine had snatched the child and rushed with it down the hill towards the Devil, a desperate terror had seized all hearts. During the terrible storm the people were trembling in fear of death, for they knew well enough in their hearts that if God's hand should come upon them and destroy them, it would be a visitation more than well deserved. When the storm was over, the news spread from house to house that the priest had brought back the baby and baptized it, but that neither Hans nor Christine had been seen.

The grey light of early morning revealed that all faces were pale, and the beautiful sun gave them no colour, for everyone knew well enough that the worst horror was yet to come. Then people heard that the priest had died covered with black tumours, and Hans was found with his terrible face, while strangely confused reports were told of Christine's transformation into the dreadful spider.

It was a fine day for harvesting, but no hands set to work; people came together as they do on the day after the day on which a great misfortune has happened. Now for the first time they truly felt in their vacillating souls what it means to consent to buy oneself off with an immortal soul from earthly trouble and distress; now they felt that there was a God in heaven Who would avenge Himself terribly for all the injustice that is done to poor children who cannot defend themselves. So they stood together trembling and whining, and anyone who was with a group felt he could not return home; but then they would begin arguing and quarrelling, the one would blame the other, everyone claimed that he had warned them and told them so earlier, and nobody minded punishment being meted out to the guilty ones, so long as he and his house might go unscathed. And if they had known of some new, innocent victim while they stood there in their terrible suspense and quarrelsome spirit, not one of them would have hesitated to make a criminal sacrifice in the hope of saving their own skins.

Then one of them shrieked out in terror in the midst of the crowd; he felt as if he had put his foot on a searing thorn, as if a red-hot nail were being driven through his foot and into the ground, as if fire were streaming through the marrow of his bones. The crowd scattered, and all eyes gazed upon the foot towards which the screaming man was reaching down with his hand. But on the foot the spider was seated, black and gross, staring poisonously and gloatingly at the people around. Then they felt the blood freezing in their veins and their breath freezing in their lungs, while their eyes were fixed in a petrified glance; the spider stared round at them quietly and maliciously, and the man's foot became black, and his body seemed as if it were a battlefield between raging fire and hissing water; fear burst the bonds of terror, and the crowd dispersed in all directions. The spider, however, had relinquished its first seat with miraculous speed, and now it crawled over this man's foot and that man's heel, so that fire pierced their bodies and their ghastly screaming impelled the others to even more hasty flight. They rushed towards their homes with the speed of the whirlwind, in dreadful fear like that of the ghostly prey pursued by the wild huntsmen, and everyone thought that the spider was at his back; they bolted their house doors behind them, but still did not stop trembling in unspeakable terror.

And one day the spider had disappeared; no fresh death screams were heard, people had to go out of their bolted houses to look for food for themselves and their cattle, deathly though their fear was. For where was the spider now, and might it not be just here and plant itself without warning on their feet? And he who walked most carefully and used his eyes most sharply was the one who found the spider suddenly sitting on his hand or his foot, running over his face, or sitting black and gross on his nose and leering into his eyes; blazing thorns dug into his limbs, the fire of hell swept over him and death laid him low.

Thus it was that the spider was now here, now there, now nowhere, now down in the valley, now up on the hills; it hissed through the grass, fell from the roof or sprang up from the ground. When people were sitting over the midday meal of porridge, it would appear gloating at the far end of the table, and before they had had time to scatter in terror the spider had run over all their hands and was sitting on the head of the father of the family, staring over the table at the blackening hands. It would fall upon people's faces at night, it would encounter them in the forest or descend upon them in the cattle shed. No one could avoid it, for it was nowhere and everywhere; no one could screen himself from it while he was awake, and when he was asleep there was no protection. When someone thought himself to be safest, in the open air or in a treetop, then fire would crawl up his back, and the spider's fiery feet could be felt in his neck as it stared over his shoulder. It spared neither infant in the cradle nor the old man on his deathbed; it was a plague more deadly than any that had been known before, and it was a form of death more terrible than any that had been previously experienced, and what was still more terrible than the death agony was the nameless fear of the spider which was everywhere and nowhere and which would suddenly be fixing its death-dealing stare on someone when he fancied that he was most secure.

The news of this terror had naturally reached the castle without delay and had brought fright and quarrelling there too, as far as such was possible within the rules of the Order. Von Stoffeln was fearful lest they themselves might receive such a visitation as had befallen their cattle earlier, and the priest who was now dead had previously said many things which now disturbed his soul. The priest had told him that all the suffering which he inflicted on the peasants would come back upon him, but he had never believed it because he thought God would know how to differentiate between a knight and a peasant, or else surely He would not have created them so differently. But in spite of this he was now afraid that things might happen as the priest had spoken; he spoke harshly to his knights and expressed the conviction that severe punishment would now befall them on account of their irresponsible words. But the knights refused to acknowledge any wrongdoing, the one passed the responsibility to the other, and even if none of them said so, they all thought that this was really von Stoffeln's affair, for if one looked at the matter straight, it was he who was answerable for everything. And after von Stoffeln, there was a young Polish knight whom they looked at askance, since he had in fact uttered the most irresponsible words about the castle and had mostly incited von Stoffeln to new building and to the presumptuous planting of the avenue of trees. This Pole, though still very young, was the wildest of them all, and if there was a rash deed to be done, he was in the lead; he was like a heathen and feared neither God nor the Devil.

He noticed clearly enough what the others thought but dared not say to him , and he noticed also their secret terror. He therefore taunted them and said, if they were afraid of a spider, what did they think they could do against dragons? Then he securely buckled on his armour and rode into the valley, swearing presumptuously that he would not return until his horse had trampled down the spider and his own fist had crushed it. Fierce hounds jumped around him, his falcon perched upon his clenched fist, his lance hung at his saddle, and the horse reared up exuberantly; those in the castle watched him ride off half spitefully, half fearfully, remembering the nightly watch on Bärhegen when the force of earthly weapons had proved so poor a defence against such an enemy.

He rode at the edge of a pine forest towards the nearest farm, peering about and above with sharp eyes. When he saw the house and the people round about, he called his hounds, made free the falcon's head and let his dagger rattle loose in its sheath. When the falcon turned its dazzled eyes to the knight, awaiting his signal, it bounded back from his fist and shot into the air; the hounds that had gathered round howled out loudly and made off into the distance with their tails between their legs. In vain the knight rode and called out, he did not see his creatures again. Then he rode towards the people in order to ask for information; they stood still until he came close. Then they shrieked out with ghastly sounds and fled into the forest and ravine, for there on the knight's helmet the spider sat black and in supernatural size, staring poisonously and malevolently across the countryside. The knight was carrying on his person the creature he was looking for, and did not realize it; in burning anger he called and rode after the people, cried out in ever greater rage, rode at an ever madder pace, yelled out ever more terribly until he and his horse plunged over a precipice down to the valley below. There his helmet and body were found, and the spider's feet had burnt through the helmet and into his brain, starting there the most fearful agony which lasted until his death.

It was after this experience that terror entered the castle in real earnest; the knights shut themselves in and still did not feel secure; they sought spiritual weapons, but for a long time they found no one who was capable of giving them guidance or who dared to venture there. At last a priest from a distant part allowed himself to be enticed there by fair words and the promise of money; he arrived and had the intention of setting out against the wicked enemy armed with holy water and holy prayers. He did not, however, strengthen himself in preparation for this with prayer and fasting, but dined with the knights early of a morning, not counting how many goblets of wine he drank and living well on venison and bear's meat. In between he talked a lot about his spiritual feats of heroism, while the knights talked about their worldly deeds, and nobody counted the number of drinks they had and the spider was forgotten. Then all at once all liveliness was extinguished, hands holding tankard or fork went numb, mouths stayed gaping, and all eyes were fixed staring at one point; von Stoffeln alone drained his tankard and went on recounting some heroic deed performed in heathen parts. But the spider sat large on his head and stared round at the knights at table, though von Stoffeln did not know this. Then pain began to pour through his brain and blood, he cried out hideously and felt his head with his hand, but the spider was no longer there, with its terrible speed it had run over all the knights' faces, and no one could prevent it; one after another shrieked out, consumed with fire, and the spider leered down from the priest's bald head into the scene of horror; the priest wanted to put out the fire which flared up first in his head and then through marrow and bone.

Only a few servants were spared in the castle, those who had never made fun of the peasants; it was they who related how terrible it had been. The feeling that the knights had what they deserved was no consolation for the peasants, whose terror became ever greater and more horrible. Many a one tried to escape. Some wanted to leave the valley, but it was precisely these who became the spider's victims. Their corpses were found strewn on the road. Others fled to the high hills, but the spider was up there before them, and when they thought they had saved themselves, there was the spider sitting on their necks or faces. The monster became more and more evil and devilish. It no longer came upon people unawares, injecting the fire of death unexpectedly; it would lurk in the grass for someone, or hang over him from a tree, staring poisonously at him. Then such a one would flee as far as his feet could carry him, and if he stood still in his breathlessness the spider would be squatting in front of him and staring poisonously at him. If he fled once more and once more had to slow down, it would again be in front of him, and only if he could flee no further did it crawl slowly up to him and kill him.

Then some people in their despair attempted resistance to see if it might not be possible to kill the spider; they threw huge stones at it when it sat before them in the grass, or hit out at it with club or axe. But it was all in vain, for the heaviest stone could not crush it nor the sharpest axe wound it; it would squat unawares on a man's face and crawl up to him unhurt. Flight, resistance, everything was in vain. At that all hope was lost, and despair filled the valley and brooded over the heights.

Up to that time there was one house only which the monster had spared and where he had never appeared; it was the house where Christine had lived and from which she had stolen the child. As the spider, she had attacked her own husband in lonely pastureland, where his corpse had been found mauled hideously as none other had been, the features distorted in unspeakable pain; it was he upon whom it had wreaked its most terrible wrath, it was the husband for whom it had prepared the most terrible final encounter. But nobody saw how it happened.

The spider had not yet come to the house; whether it was saving it up till last or whether it was afraid of approaching it, nobody could guess.

But fear had entered there no less than at other places.

The devout woman had recovered her health and had no fear on her own account, but was considerably afraid for her faithful little boy and his little sister; she watched over them day and night, and the faithful grandmother shared her cares and her vigilance. And together they prayed God that He might keep their eyes open as they were on the watch and that He would illumine and strengthen them so that they might save the innocent children.

As they kept watch through the long nights it often seemed to them as if they could see the spider glimmering and glittering in a dark corner, or as if it were peering in at them through the window; then their fear increased, for they knew no way of protecting the children from the spider, and so they prayed the more ardently to God for His counsel and support. They had collected all kinds of weapons to have handy, but when they heard that the stone lost its heaviness and the axe its sharpness, they put them aside again. Then the idea came to the mother more and more clearly and vividly that if someone would dare to grasp the spider with his hand, it would be possible to overcome it. She had also heard of people who, when stone-throwing proved useless, had attempted to crush the spider in their hands, though without success. A fearful stream of fire which convulsed through hand and arm destroyed all strength and brought death to the heart. It seemed to her that if she could not succeed in crushing the spider, she might well be able to grasp hold of it, and God would lend her sufficient strength to put it away in some place where it would be harmless. She had already often heard tell of knowledgeable men imprisoning demons in a hole in a cliff or in wood which they had closed with a peg, and so long as no one pulled out the peg, the demon would have to remain pinned down in the hole.

The spirit moved her more and more to attempt something similar herself. She bored a hole in the window post which was nearest to her at her right hand as she sat by the cradle; she prepared a peg which fitted closely into the hole, blessed it with holy water, put out a hammer and prayed day and night to God for strength to accomplish the deed. But sometimes the flesh was stronger than the spirit, and heavy sleep pressed on her eyes; then she saw the spider in her dreams, leering at her little boy's golden hair, then she started up out of her dream and touched her boy's locks. But there was no spider there, and a smile played on his little face in the way children smile when they see their angel in a dream, but the mother seemed to see the spider's poisonous eyes glittering in every corner of the room, and for a long time she could not go to sleep.

In this way sleep had once overcome her after she had been keeping strict watch, and it encircled her closely. Then it appeared to her as if the pious priest, who had died saving her child, were rushing up to her from far spaces and were calling to her from the distance: 'Wake up, woman, the enemy is here!' He called thus three times, and it was not until the third time that she wrested herself from the tight bonds of sleep, but as she wearily raised her heavy eyelids, she saw the spider, swollen with poison, crawling slowly up to the little bed towards the face of her boy. Then she thought of God and seized the spider with rapid grasp. Then streams of fire emanated from the spider, piercing the faithful mother through hand and arm to her heart, but motherly fidelity and motherly love made her keep her hand tightly closed, and God gave her strength to hold out. Amid thousandfold pains of death she forced the spider with her one hand into the hole that had been prepared, and with the other hand she pressed the peg over the hole and then hammered it fast.

Inside there was a roaring and a raging as when whirlwinds struggle with the sea, the house swayed on its foundations, but the peg held fast and the spider remained imprisoned. The faithful mother, however, was still overjoyed that she had saved her children; she thanked God for His grace, then she too died the same death as all the others, but her motherly fidelity blotted out the pains, and the angels accompanied her soul to God's throne, where all heroes are who have given their lives for others and risked everything for the sake of God and their beloved ones.

Now the Black Death was at an end. Peace and life came back to the valley. The black spider was seen no more at that time, for it stayed imprisoned in that hole, where it remains still now."

"What, in that black piece of wood there?" the godmother cried, starting up from the ground in one movement as if she had been sitting on an anthill. She had been sitting against that piece of wood when she had been inside the room. And now her back was burning, she turned round, she looked behind her, felt over herself with her hand and could not escape from the fear that the black spider was sitting on her neck.

The others also felt their hearts constricted after the grandfather had finished talking. A great silence had come over them. Nobody cared to venture a joke, nor did anyone feel inclined to assent to the story; each preferred to listen for the first word of the other so that they could adjust their own remarks accordingly, for that is the easiest way to avoid making mistakes. Then the midwife came running along; she had called to them several times already without getting an answer, and her face burned deep red; it was as if the spider had been crawling about on it. She began to scold them because nobody would come, however loudly she might call. That really did seem to her to be a queer business; when the food was all ready, nobody would come to the table, and if after all it was spoilt, they would say it was all her fault; she knew well enough how these things happened. Nobody could eat fat meat like that indoors once it had gone cold – and anyway it wouldn't be good for them to do so.

Now the people did come, but quite slowly, and none of them was willing to be the first at the door; the grandfather had to go first. This time it was not so much the usual custom of not wanting to give the impression that they could not wait to get at the food; it was the hesitation which befalls all people when they stand at the entrance to a gruesome place, though really there was nothing gruesome inside. The handsome decanters of wine, freshly filled, gleamed brightly on the table; two sleek hams shone forth; mighty roast joints of veal and mutton were steaming; fresh Bernese cakes lay between the dishes of meat, plates of fritters and plates with three kinds of cake on them had been squeezed in between, and the pots of sweetened tea were not missing either. Thus it was a lovely sight, and yet they all paid little attention to it, but instead they all looked round with frightened glances, wondering if the spider might not be glittering out of some corner or even be staring down at them from the magnificent ham with its poisonous eyes. It could not be seen anywhere, and yet nobody paid the usual compliments ("What were they thinking, to go on putting so much in front of them? Whoever was going to eat it? They'd already had more than enough"), but everybody crowded down to the lower end of the table and nobody wanted to be at the top.

It was useless asking the guests to come to the top end of the table and to point to the empty places there; they stood at the bottom end as if nailed there. In vain the father of the newborn child poured out the wine and called to them to come along and drink a health, it was all ready. Then he took the godmother by the arm and said, "You be the most sensible and set an example!" But the godmother resisted with all her strength, and that was not little, saying, "I'm not going to sit up there again, not for a thousand pounds! I can feel something stinging up and down my back, as if somebody were playing about it with nettles. And if I sat over there by the window frame, I should feel the terrible spider on my neck all the time."

"That's your fault, grandfather," the grandmother said. "Why do you bring up such subjects! That sort of thing does no good these days and can only do harm to the whole house and family. And if one day the children come home from school crying and complaining that the other children have been baiting them that their grandmother was a witch and was shut up in the window post, well, that'll be your fault."

"Be quiet, grandmother!" the grandfather said. "Nowadays everything soon gets forgotten again and nobody keeps things long in their memory, as they used to. They wanted to hear about the business from me, and it is better for people to hear the exact truth rather than to make something up for themselves; truth can bring our house no dishonour. But come and sit down! Look, I'll sit down myself in front of the peg in the window post. After all, I've sat there many thousands of days already without fear or hesitation, and therefore without danger. Only if ever evil thoughts happened to rise within me which could give the Devil a hold, I had the feeling that there was a purring behind me, like a cat purring when you play with it and stroke its fur and it feels comfortable, and I had a queer, strange feeling up my back. But otherwise the spider keeps itself as still as a mouse inside there, and so long as we here outside do not forget God, it has to go on waiting within."

Then the guests took heart and sat down, but nobody moved up really close to the grandfather. Now at last the father could begin serving; he placed a mighty piece of roast meat on his neighbour the godmother's plate and she cut a small piece off and placed what remained on her neighbour's plate, removing it from her fork with her thumb. In this manner the piece of meat was passed on, until someone said he thought he would keep it now, for there would certainly be more where that piece came from; a new piece now began the rounds. While the father was pouring out wine and serving, and the guests were telling him what a busy day he was having today, the midwife went round with the sweet tea, which was strongly spiced with saffron and cinnamon, and offered it to everybody, saying that if anybody was fond of it, all they had to do was to say so, it was there for everybody. And if anyone said he did like it, she poured tea into his wine, saying she was fond of it too, it made it easier to stand up to the wine and didn't give you a headache. They ate and drank. But scarcely was the noise over, which always occurs when people are sitting behind new dishes of food, when everyone became quiet again, and faces grew serious: it was clear that all thoughts were turned to the spider. Eyes glanced shyly and furtively at the peg behind the grandfather's back, and yet everyone was reluctant to take up the subject again.

Then the godmother cried out loud and almost fell off her chair. A fly had passed over the peg, she had believed that the spider's black legs were creeping out of the hole, and her whole body trembled with terror. People hardly had time to make fun of her, for her fright was a welcome reason for beginning to talk afresh about the spider, and once a matter has really touched our mind, it does not easily let it go again.

"But listen here, cousin," the elder godfather said. "Hasn't the spider ever got out of the hole since then? Has it always stayed inside all these hundreds of years?"

"Oh," the grandmother said, "it would be better to be quiet about the whole business." After all, they had been talking the whole afternoon about it.

"Oh, Mother," the cousin said, "you let your old man talk, he's been entertaining us very well, and nobody will hold the business against you, after all you're not descended from Christine. And you won't succeed in turning our thoughts away from the subject; and if we're not allowed to talk about it, we shan't talk about anything else, and then we shan't be entertained any more. Now, grandfather, come and talk, your old woman won't begrudge it us!"

"Oh, if you want to insist, you can, as far as I am concerned, but it would have been more sensible to have started on something different now, and specially now that night is on the way," the grandmother said.

Then the grandfather began, and all faces became tense once more.

"What I know isn't much more now, but I will tell you what I do know; perhaps somebody can take a lesson from it in our own day; it really wouldn't do any harm to quite a lot of folk.

When people knew that the spider had been shut in and that their lives were safe again, it is said that they felt as if they were in heaven and as if the dear God with His blessedness were in the midst of them, and for a long time things went well. They held fast to God and shunned the Devil, and the knights who had arrived at the castle as newcomers also stood in awe of God's hand and treated the people gently and helped them to recover.

But everybody regarded this house with reverence, almost as if it were a church. Admittedly the sight of it made them shudder at first, when they saw the prison of the terrible spider and thought how easily it might break out from there and start the whole wretchedness afresh with the Devil's violence. But they soon saw that God's strength was greater than the Devil's, and out of gratitude to the mother who had died for them all, they helped the children and worked the farm for them for nothing, until they were able to look after it themselves. The knights were willing to allow them to build a new house so that they need have no fear of the spider, in case this latter might accidentally be set free in a house which was inhabited, and offers of help came from many neighbours who could not get rid of their fear of the monster which had made them tremble so much. But the grandmother would not hear of it.

She taught her grandchildren that it was here that the spider had been imprisoned in the name of God the Father, Son and Holy Spirit; as long as the three holy names held sway in the house and as long as food and drink were blessed in the three holy names at this table, they would be safe from the spider and the spider would be secure in the hole and no accident could make its imprisonment less secure. As they sat at the table with the spider behind them, they would never forget how necessary God was to them nor how mighty He was; in this way the spider would remind them of God, and in spite of the Devil it would be a means to their salvation. But if they forsook God, even if this happened a hundred hours' walk away from there, the spider or the Devil himself would be able to find them. The children understood this, remained living in the house, grew up to be God-fearing, and the blessing of God was over the house.

The little boy who had been so faithful to the mother, just as his mother had been faithful to him, grew up into a fine man who was beloved of God and men and found favour with the knights. Therefore he was also blessed with worldly goods and never forgot God because of this, he never became grasping in his prosperity; he helped others in their need, just as he wished that he might be helped in the last resort; and where he was too weak to give help himself, he became all the more forceful an intercessor with God and men. He was blessed with a good wife, and between them there was a deep and secure peace, and therefore their children flourished and became virtuous, and both found a quiet death after a long life. His family continued to flourish in the fear of God and in right living.

Truly the blessing of God lay over the whole valley, and there was prosperity in the fields and the cattle sheds and peace among men. The terrible lesson had gone to people's hearts, and they held fast to God; whatever they did, they did in His name, and where one man could help another, he did not hesitate to do so. No evil, but only good came to them from the castle. Fewer and fewer knights lived there, for the fighting in heathen parts became ever harder, and every hand that could wield a sword became more and more essential; but those who were in the castle were reminded daily by the great hall of death, where the spider had asserted its power over knights just as elsewhere over peasants, that God rules with the same strength over all who fall away from Him, whether they are knights or peasants.

In this way many years passed in happiness and blessing, and this valley became celebrated above all others. Its houses were impressive, its stocks were large, many a gold coin lay in the coffers, its cattle were the finest over hill and dale, its daughters were renowned up and down the country and its sons welcomed everywhere. But just as the pear tree which is best nourished and has the strongest growth is the one into which the canker penetrates, consuming it until it withers and dies, so it happens that where God's stream of blessing flows most richly over men, canker comes into the blessing, puffs the people up and makes them blind, until they forget God because of the blessing, forget Him Who has given the wealth on account of the wealth itself, until they become like the Israelites who forgot God, after He had helped them, on account of the golden calf.

Thus after many generations had passed, pride and arrogance made their home in the valley, brought there and increased by women from other parts. Clothes became more pretentious, jewels could be seen gleaming on them, and indeed pride dared to display itself even on the holy implements themselves, and

89

instead of people's hearts being directed in prayer fervently to God, their eyes lingered arrogantly on the golden beads of their rosaries. Thus their public worship became pomp and pride, though their hearts became hardened towards God and man. There was little concern for God's commandments, and His service and His servants were scorned; for where there is much arrogance or much money the delusion willingly enters which thinks selfish desires to be wisdom and values this worldly wisdom higher than God's wisdom. Just as the peasants had in earlier days been ill treated by the knights, now they in their turn became hard towards their servants and ill-treated them, and the less they themselves worked, the more they expected from their servants, and the more work they demanded from farmhands and maids, the more they treated them like senseless cattle, not thinking that their servants too had souls to be taken care of. Where there is much money and pride, people start building, one farmer vying with another, and just as the knights had used to build earlier, the peasant farmers were now building, and just as the knights had ill used them in earlier times, now they were merciless to their servants and their cattle, once the craze for building came over them. This change of outlook had also come over this house, although the old wealth had remained.

Almost two hundred years had passed since the spider had been made prisoner in the hole. At that time a cunning and overbearing woman was mistress here; she did not come from Lindau, but all the same resembled Christine in many respects. She too came from a distant part and was addicted to vanity and pride, and she had an only son; her husband had died through her domineering spirit. This son was a handsome fellow, good-natured and friendly to man and beast; she in her turn was very fond of him, but she did not let him notice it. She domineered over him at every step he took, and none of his friends would be tolerated by her unless she had first given her approval, and he had long been grown up, but still was not allowed to go with the village youth or to go to a local fair without his mother's company. When at last she thought he was old enough, she gave him as a wife one of her relations, a woman after her own heart. Now he had two masters instead of only one, and both were equally proud and arrogant, and because they were like this, they wanted Christen to be like this too, and whenever he was friendly and humble, as suited him so well, he soon learnt who was master.

For a long time the old house had been a thorn in their eyes and they were ashamed of it, since the neighbours had new houses although they were scarcely as rich as they were. The legend of the spider and what the grandmother had said was at that time still in everyone's memory, otherwise the old house would have been torn down long ago, but everybody resisted the two women in this. The latter, however, came more and more to interpret this resistance as envy which begrudged them a new house. In addition, they came to feel more and more uneasy in the old house. Whenever they sat at the table here, they felt either as if the cat were purring complacently behind them or else as if the hole were gradually opening and the spider taking aim at their necks. They lacked the faithful spirit which had closed up the hole, and therefore they were more and more afraid that the hole might open. Consequently they thought they had found a good reason for building a new house, since in the new house they would not have to be afraid of the spider. They wanted to hand over the old house to the servants, who often were an obstacle to their vanity, and in this way they came to their decision.

Christen was very unwilling to do this; he knew what the old grandmother had said and believed that the family blessing was linked to the family house, and he was not afraid of the spider, and when he sat up here at the table, it seemed to him as if he could pray most reverently. He said how he felt, but his womenfolk told him to be quiet, and because he was their servant, he did keep quiet, but he often wept bitterly when they were not there to see him.

Up there, beyond the tree under which we were sitting, a house was to be built, a house the like of which nobody else in the district possessed. In presumptuous impatience, because they knew nothing about building and could not wait to show off with their new house, they maltreated workmen and animals during the building process and did not even rest on holy feast days and begrudged the workers their rest even at night; there was no neighbour with whom they were satisfied, however much help he might give them, no neighbour whom they did not wish ill when he went home to look after his own affairs after he had given them free assistance, as was the custom even at that time.

When they started building and drove the first peg into the threshold, smoke rose from the hole like damp straw when it is set alight; at that the workpeople shook their heads with misgiving and said, both secretly and aloud, that the new building would not become old; but the women laughed at this and took no notice of the sign that had been given. When finally the house had been built, they moved in and furnished it with unheard-of luxury, and for a housewarming gave a party that lasted three days, so that children and grandchildren still talked about it throughout the whole Emmental.

But it is said that all the three days long a strange humming could be heard in the whole house like the purring of a cat that is contented to have its fur stroked. But they could not find the cat from which the purring came, for all they searched everywhere; then many a one felt ill at ease, and in spite of all the munificence he would slip off in the midst of the celebrations. It was only the two women who heard nothing or else took notice of nothing; they thought that now the new house was there they had nothing to lose.

Yes, a blind man does not even see the sun, nor does a deaf man hear thunder. Consequently the women of the house were delighted, grew more presumptuous every day, did not think of the spider, but lived in the new house a luxurious, indolent life, dolling themselves up and overeating; there was nobody like them, they thought, and they did not think of God.

The servants stayed on by themselves in the old house, living as they liked, and when Christen wanted to keep the old house under his surveillance, the women would not tolerate this and railed at him, the mother chiefly out of vanity, the wife mainly out of jealousy. Consequently there was no order down there in the old house and soon no fear of God either, and where there is no master in control, that is what usually happens. If there is no master sitting at the head of the table, no master listening alertly in the house, no master holding the reins both within and outside, then the fellow who behaves most wildly thinks he is the greatest and the man who talks most recklessly thinks he is the best.

That is how things went in the house down below, and all the servants soon resembled a pack of cats when they are at their wildest. Nobody knew anything more about praying, and therefore there was respect neither for God's will nor God's gifts. Just as the arrogance of the two mistresses no longer knew any bounds, so the animal insolence of the servants knew no limits. They audaciously spoilt the bread, they threw porridge over the table with spoons at each other's heads and they even defiled the food in bestial manner in order maliciously to take away the others' enjoyment of their food. They provoked the neighbours, tormented the cattle, jeered at all divine worship, denied all higher authority and abused in all manner of ways the priest who had spoken to them admonishingly; in short, they no longer had any fear of God or man and behaved more wildly every day. The farmhands and the maids lived most dissolutely, and yet they tormented one another wherever possible, and when the farmhands could not think of any new way of tormenting the maids, one of them had the idea of terrifying or taming the maids with the threat of the spider in the hole. He slung spoonfuls of porridge or milk up against the peg and shouted out that the spider inside must be hungry as it had had nothing to eat for so many centuries. At that the maids shrieked aloud and promised everything that they could, and even the other farmhands felt a shudder of horror.

As the game was repeated without any punishment ensuing, it lost its effect; the maids no longer cried out or made any promises, and the other farmhands also began the same game. Now this particular fellow began to go at the hole with his knife, swearing the most horrible oaths that he would loosen the peg and see what was inside, for it was time they had something new to see. This aroused new horror, and the fellow who did this was master of them all and could compel them, especially the maids, to do whatever he wanted.

Indeed this man is said to have been a really strange fellow, and nobody knew where he came from. He could behave as gently as a lamb and as fiercely as a wolf; if he were on his own with a woman he was a gentle lamb, but in the company at large he was like a ravening wolf and behaved as if he hated everyone, as if he wanted to outdo them all in wild deeds and words – but men like that are supposed to be just the most attractive ones to women. That is why the maids were shocked at him in public, but are said to have liked him best of all when alone with him. His eyes were uneven, but it was impossible to say what colour they were, and the two eyes disliked one another, for they never looked in the same direction, but he knew how to conceal this with long hair over his eyes and by humbly looking down to the ground. His hair was beautifully waved, but it was difficult to say whether it was red or blonde; in the shade it was the most beautiful flaxen hair, but when the sun shone on it, no squirrel's coat was redder. He tormented the cattle worse than anybody else. The cattle in their turn hated him also. Each of the farmhands thought that he was his friend, and yet he would set them up one against the other. He was the only one of them who suited the two mistresses, and was the only one who was often in the upper house; then the maids behaved wildly in the house below; as soon as he observed this, he would stick his knife into the peg and begin his threatening, until the maids ate humble pie.

However, this game too did not continue to be effective for long. The maids became used to it and finally said: 'Do it then, if you dare – but you daren't!'

The holy eve of Christmas was approaching. They had no thought for the meaning of Christmas and had planned to have a wildly merry time. In the castle over yonder only an old knight lived now; a rogue of a bailiff administered everything to his own advantage. They had procured a noble Hungarian wine from him by means of conniving at a piece of roguery (the knights were engaged in hard fighting in Hungary), and they did not know the strength and fire of the noble wine. A terrible storm arose, with thunder and lightning, such as you very rarely see at this time of year, and it was so fierce that you could not have rooted out a dog from under the stove. It did not stop them going to church, because they would not have gone there even in fine weather and would have let the master go there on his own, but this fact prevented others from visiting them, so that they now were alone in the old house with the noble wine.

They began the holy Christmas Eve with swearing and dancing and with even wilder and more wicked things; then they sat down to the meal, for which the maids had cooked meat, white sauce and any other good things they could steal. Then their coarseness became ever more repulsive, they defiled all the food and blasphemed against everything holy; the farmhand mentioned before made fun of the priest, divided out bread and drank his wine as if he were officiating at mass, baptized the dog under the stove and carried on until the others became anxious and fearful, ruthless as they might otherwise be. Then he stabbed into the hole with his knife and said with curses that he would show them very different things. When they refused to be scared by this, because he had done this sort of thing so often before and there was not much to be gained by driving the knife against the peg, he grasped a gimlet in his half-crazy fury, swore in the most terrible language until their hair stood on end that he would show them what he could do and make them regret laughing at him, then he screwed the gimlet with fierce turns into the peg. The rest fell upon him crying out loudly, but before anyone could prevent it, he laughed like the Devil himself and gave the gimlet a violent wrench.

Then the whole house rocked under a monstrous thunder-clap, the evildoer was flung onto his back, a red stream of fire broke out from the hole and there in the middle sat the spider, huge and black, swollen with the poison of centuries, gloating in poisonous glee over the criminals who were benumbed in deadly fear and could not move a limb to escape from the terrible monster that crept slowly and malevolently over their faces and injected into them a fiery death.

Then the house quivered with terrible howls of pain such as a hundred wolves together cannot emit even when they are gnawed by hunger. And soon a similar cry of pain sounded from the new house, and Christen, just coming up the hill from holy mass, thought that thieves must have broken in, and, trusting his strong arm, he rushed to help his family. He did not find thieves, but death: his wife and his mother were wrestling with death and already had no more voice in their heavily swollen, black faces; his children were sleeping quietly, and their carefree faces were healthy and ruddy. There arose in Christen a terrible suspicion of what had happened; he rushed into the lower house where he saw the servants all lying dead, their living room turned into a death chamber, the fearful hole in the window post opened wide, and he saw the gimlet in the terribly contorted hand of the farmhand and the dreadful peg on the point of the gimlet. Now he knew what had happened, struck his hands together above his head, and if the earth could have swallowed him up, this would have suited him well. Then something crept out from behind the stove and nestled close to him; he started in terror, but it was not the spider, it was a poor boy whom he had taken into the house out of charity and had then left among the ruthless servants, as indeed often happens even nowadays, when people take in children in the name of God and then let them go to the Devil. This boy had taken no part in the evil behaviour of the servants and had fled in terror behind the stove; the spider had spared him alone, and now he could relate what had happened.

But even as the boy was speaking, cries of terror sounded across from other houses, in spite of the wind and the weather. The spider sped through the valley as if with the pent-up lust of centuries, picking out first the most sumptuous houses where people thought of God least and the world most and therefore least cared to know about death.

Already before daybreak the news was in every house that the old spider had broken loose and was once more bringing death to the community; it was said that many already lay dead and that further down in the valley cry upon cry was being raised to heaven from those who had been branded and now had to die. You can imagine now what distress there was in the district, what fear in all hearts and what a Christmas this was in Sumiswald! Not a soul could think of the joy which Christmas usually brings, and such distress came from the criminal behaviour of men. But every day the distress grew, for the spider was now quicker and more poisonous than the previous time. Now it was at one end of the parish, now at the other; it appeared at the same time on the hills and in the valley. If on the previous occasion it had for the most part given the mark of death here to one person and there to another, this time it seldom left a house before it had poisoned all who were living there; it was not until all the inmates were writhing in agony of death that the spider sat upon the threshold and gloated maliciously over the havoc of its poisoning, as if to say that here it was, and it had come back again, however long its term of imprisonment might have been.

It was as if the spider knew that little time was to be allowed it, or as if it wanted to save itself trouble; it killed many people off at once, wherever it could. That is why it liked to lie lurking for the passing of the processions of people who wished to accompany the dead to church. Now here, now there, for preference down at the Kilchstalden, it appeared in the midst of a crowd of people or else suddenly glared down from the coffin at the mourners. Then a terrible cry of distress rose to heaven from the procession of mourners, man after man collapsed, until the whole line of mourners lay in the road wrestling with death, until there was no more life among them and a heap of dead lay around the coffin, as bold warriors lie round their flag when overcome by greater forces. After that no more dead were brought to the church, for nobody wanted to carry or escort them; where death seized them, there they were left lying.

Despair lay over the whole valley. Anger was fierce in all hearts, pouring out in terrible imprecations against poor Christen, for he was held responsible for everything. Now all at once everybody was certain that Christen should not have gone from the old house and left the servants to their own devices. All at once everybody knew that a master is more or less responsible for his servants and should set himself against godless living, godless talking and godless defilement of the gifts of God. Now all at once everybody had lost their vanity and arrogance, relegating their vices to the lowest depths of hell; they would scarcely have believed God Himself if He had told them that until a few days ago they had borne these vices within themselves. They were all pious again, wore their poorest clothes, carried their old, despised rosaries in their hands and persuaded themselves that they had always been as pious as this and that it was not their fault if they could not persuade God in the same way. Christen alone among them all was deemed to be godless, and curses fell upon him like mountains from all sides. And yet he was perhaps the best of them, except that his will lay bound by that of his womenfolk, and such dependence is certainly a heavy sin for any man, and a man cannot escape the weight of responsibility because he is different from what God intends him to be. Christen realized this too, and therefore he was not defiant or loud, but assumed more guilt than was rightly his; but he did not reconcile people by this, for indeed it was at this point that they cried to one another how great his sin must be, since he took so much upon himself and was so submissive, indeed even confessed that he was worthless.

He, however, prayed day and night to God that He might turn the evil away, but it became more terrible from day to day. He realized that he must make good where he had fallen short, that he must sacrifice himself and that the deed which his ancestress had performed was now to fall to him. He prayed to God until the resolve grew right ardently in his heart that he must save the valley community and atone for the evil; his resolve was strengthened by steady courage that does not waver and is always ready for the same deed, in the morning as in the evening.

So he moved with his children out of the old house into the new one, cut a new peg for the hole, had it hallowed with holy water and prayers, placed the hammer by the peg, sat down by the children's beds and waited for the spider.

Seated there, he prayed, watched and wrestled with firm courage against the heaviness of sleep, and did not falter; but the spider did not come, although it was everywhere else, for the plague became more and more deadly, and the rage of the survivors ever wilder.

In the midst of these terrors a wild woman was expecting to give birth to a child. Then people were overwhelmed by the old fear that the spider might take the child unbaptized, the pledge of the old agreement. The woman behaved as if insane and had no trust in God, but had all the more hatred and revenge in her heart.

It was known how in the old days people had protected themselves against the green huntsman, and how the priest was the shield whom they had placed between themselves and the eternal fiend. It was decided now to send for the priest, but who should be the messenger? The unburied dead, whom the spider had stricken during the funeral processions, barred the roads, and would any messenger going over the deserted heights to fetch the priest be able to escape the spider who seemed to know everything? Everyone was hesitant. Then at last the woman's husband thought that if the spider would be seizing him, it would be as likely to get hold of him in his own home as on the road; if he were doomed to die, he would not escape death here any more than there.

He set out on the way, but hour after hour went by, and no messenger came back. Rage and distress became more and more terrible, and the hour of the birth drew closer and closer. Then in the fury of despair the woman raised herself from her bed, lurched out towards the house of Christen, who had been the object of thousandfold curses and who sat in prayer by his children, awaiting the encounter with the spider. Already from afar her screaming could be heard, and her imprecations thundered on Christen's door long before she wrenched it open to bring the storm of her revilement to him in his room. When she rushed in with so terrible an appearance, he started up, wondering at first whether this might not be Christine in her original shape. But as she stood in the doorway, pain held back her walk, and she clung to the doorpost, pouring out the flood of her curses upon poor Christen. He should be the messenger, she said, unless he wished to be cursed with his children and children's children for all time and eternity. At that, pain smothered her swearing, and a little son was born to the wild woman on Christen's threshold, and all who had followed her fled in all directions, expecting the worst to happen. Christen held the innocent child in his arms; the woman's eyes stared, piercing, fierce and poisonous at him from her distorted features, and he felt more and more as if she herself were the spider. Then the power of God came upon him, and a superhuman willpower became mighty within him; he threw an intense, loving glance at his children, wrapped the newborn infant in his warm cloak, strode over the fiercely staring woman down the hill and along the valley towards Sumiswald. He made up his mind to take the child to its holy baptism, in expiation of the guilt which lay upon him as head of his house; the rest he would leave to God. Dead bodies hindered his progress, and he had to be careful where he put his feet. Then light-moving feet caught him up; it was the poor boy who felt afraid to be with the wild woman and who, impelled by a childish urge, had run after his master. Christen's heart felt pierced as if by thorns to think that his children were left alone with the raging woman. However, his feet did not stay still, but pressed on to their holy destination.

He had already got down to the Kilchstalden and the shrine was in sight, when there was a sudden gleaming before him in the middle of the road, there was movement in the bushes, the spider sat in the road, a feather was waving red from behind a bush, and the spider reared up high as if to spring. Then Christen called with a loud voice to God in Three Persons, and a wild shout sounded from the bushes, the red feather disappeared, he placed the infant in the boy's arms and after commending his soul to the Lord he seized with a strong hand the spider which, as if transfixed by the holy words, remained motionless in the same spot. Fire streamed through his limbs, but he held fast; the road was free, and the boy with understanding mind hastened to the priest with the child. But Christen, with fire in his strong hand, hurried with winged course towards his own house. The burning in his hand was terrible, the spider's poison penetrated through all his limbs. His blood became fire. His strength was on the verge of being benumbed, and his breathing almost stopped, but he prayed on and on, kept God firmly before his mind's eye and held out in the fire of hell. Already now he could see his house; as the pain grew, so did his hope, and there at the door was the woman. When the latter saw him coming without her child, she rushed at him like a tigress that has been robbed of her young, believing him responsible for the most shameful betrayal. She took no notice of his gesticulations, did not hear the words coming from his heaving breast, rushed into his outstretched hands and clung on to them; in deathly fear he was compelled to drag the raging woman into the house with him. He has to fight his arms free before he succeeds in forcing the spider back into the old house and securing the peg with dying hands. With God's help he is able to do it. He throws his dying glance at his children as they lie sweetly smiling in their sleep. Then he feels at rest, a higher hand seems to extinguish the fire within him, and praying aloud he closes his eyes in readiness for death. Those who ventured in, cautiously and fearfully, to see what had happened to the woman, found serenity and joy on his face. They were astonished to see the hole closed up, but they found the woman lying burnt and distorted in death; she had found fiery death from Christen's hand. While they were standing by without knowing what had happened, the boy came back carrying the child, and with him was the priest who had quickly christened the child according to the custom of the time and was ready to go, well-armed and courageously, to the same struggle in which his predecessor had given up his life in victory. But God did not require such a sacrifice from this priest, for another man had already fought the fight.

For a long time people did not understand what a great deed Christen had accomplished. When at last faith and insight came to them, they prayed joyfully with the priest and thanked God for the life given to them anew and for the strength which He had given to Christen. They begged Christen's forgiveness for their injustice towards him, although he was now dead, and resolved to bury him with high honours, and his memory became gloriously enshrined in their souls like that of a saint. They hardly knew how they felt when this so fearful terror which had been coursing through their limbs suddenly disappeared and they could look joyously up again into the blue sky without fear that the spider was meanwhile crawling on their feet. They decided to have many masses sung and to hold a general procession to the church; above all they wanted to perform the funeral obsequies for the two bodies of Christen and the woman who had pressed upon him, and after that the other corpses were also to find a resting ground, as far as possible.

It was a solemn day when the whole valley walked to the church, and there were solemn feelings in many hearts, many sins were confessed, many vows were sworn, and from that day on much of the old pretentiousness disappeared from people's faces and clothes.

After many tears had been shed in the church and in the churchyard, and after many prayers had been offered, all the people from the valley community who had come to the funeral – and all had come who had the use of their limbs – went to the inn for the customary refreshment. It now happened there that, as usual, women and children sat at their own table, while all the grown men could be seated round the famous round table which may still now be seen at the Bear Inn at Sumiswald. This table was preserved in remembrance of the fact that once there were only a couple of dozen men in a community where now nearly two thousand live, in remembrance of the fact that the lives of the two thousand are also kept in the hand of Him Who saved the two dozen. On that occasion people did not linger at the funeral meal; hearts were too full for there to be room for much food and drink. When they came out of the village onto the open heights above, they saw a red glow in the sky, and when they came home they found the new house burned to the ground; how it happened, they never found out.

But people did not forget what Christen had done for them, and they repaid his deed to his children. They brought these children up piously and sturdily in the most God-fearing household; nobody took any liberties with the children's property, although no legal account was to be seen. Their property was increased and well looked after, and when the children had grown up, they had been cheated neither of their worldly goods nor of their souls. They became righteous, God-fearing persons who enjoyed both the grace of God and the favour of men, and who found blessing in this life and even more in the sight of heaven. And so it remained in the family, and there was no fear of the spider, since there was fear of God, and as it was, so may it remain, if God wills it, as long as there is a house standing here and as long as children follow their parents in action and in thought."

Here the grandfather was silent, and for a long time all were silent, and some were pondering over what they had heard, and the others thought he must be taking breath and then be going to continue further.

105

At last the elder godfather said: "I have often sat at the round table and have heard of the plague, and how after this all the men in the parish could find room to sit round it. But just how it all happened, nobody could tell me. Some talked one sort of nonsense and others another sort. But tell me, where did you hear all this?"

"Oh," the grandfather said, "it was passèd down in our family from father to son, and when the memory of it was lost among other people in the valley, it was kept very dark in the family and they were reluctant to let people know anything of it. It was only talked about inside the family, so that no member should forget what it is that builds a house and destroys it, that brings blessing and takes it away. You can tell from the way my old woman talks how she dislikes it being talked about so openly. But it seems to me that the longer time goes on, the more necessary it is to talk about it to show how far people can go in arrogance and pride. That is why I don't make such a secret of the business any longer, and it isn't the first time that I have told the story to good friends. I also think that what has preserved our family in happiness for so many years will not do harm to others either, and that it isn't right to make a secret of what brings prosperity and God's blessing."

"You are right, cousin," the godfather answered. "But there is one thing I must ask you all the same: was the house which you pulled down seven years ago the original old one? I find it hard to believe that."

"No," the grandfather said. "The old house had already become dilapidated almost three hundred years ago, and for a long time even then there had not been room in it for God's blessings from the fields and meadows. And yet the family did not want to leave it, and they dared not build a new one, for they had not forgotten what had happened to the earlier one. Thus they came into a very embarrassing situation and finally asked the advice of a wise man who is said to have lived at Haslebach. He is said to have replied that they might certainly build a new house on the site of the old one and nowhere else, but that they must be certain to preserve two things, the old piece of wood in which the spider was kept, and the old strength of mind which had imprisoned the spider into the old piece of wood; then the old blessing would be present also in the new house.

"They built the new house and with prayer and care inserted the old piece of wood into the structure, and the spider did not move, and the spirit in the family and the blessing upon it did not change.

"But the new house also became old and small in its turn, its woodwork became worm-eaten and rotten, and only the post here remained firm and hard as iron. My father already should have built anew, but he could avoid doing so, and so it came to my turn. After long hesitation I ventured to take this step. I did as people earlier had done and inserted the old piece of wood into the new house, and the spider did not move. But I am willing to admit that I never prayed so ardently in my whole life as when I was holding the fateful piece of wood in my hands; my hand, my whole body was burning, and unconsciously I had to look whether black marks might not be growing on my hand and body, and a mountainous weight fell from my mind when everything was at last in its place. Then my conviction grew even stronger that neither I nor my children and my children's children would have to fear anything from the spider, so long as we fear God."

Then the grandfather was silent, and the others still felt the shudder that had run up their backs when they heard that the grandfather had had the piece of wood in his hands, and they thought how they would feel if they too had had to take it in their hands.

At last the cousin said: "The only thing is that it's a pity you can't know how much of this sort of thing is true. You can hardly believe everything, and yet there must be some truth about the matter, or else the old piece of wood would not be there."

The younger godfather said that you could learn a lot from it, whether it was all true or not, and what was more, they had also been enthralled by the story; it seemed to him as if he had just come out of church.

They shouldn't say too much about it, the grandmother said, or else her old man would start on another story; now they should get on and have something to eat and drink, it was indeed a shame the way nobody was eating or drinking. After all it couldn't all be bad, they had done as well as they knew how with the cooking.

Now there was much eating and drinking, and in between many a sensible conversation took place, until the moon stood large and golden in the sky, the stars stepped out from their chambers to remind the men that it was time for them too to go to their rooms to sleep.

Although they saw well enough the secret reminders in the sky, the people were sitting there so cosily and each of them felt his heart beating uncannily when he thought of the journey home, and even if nobody said so, it was true that none of them wanted to be the first to go.

At last the godmother stood up and with trembling heart made preparations to leave, but she was not without reliable companions, and the whole company departed together from the hospitable house with many thanks and good wishes, in spite of all requests, made to individuals and to the whole party, that they could surely stay a bit longer, it wasn't really dark yet.

Soon it was still outside the house; soon too it was still inside. Peacefully the house lay there, gleaming the length of the valley, clean and beautiful in the light of the moon; with friendly care it concealed good people in sweet sleep, the sleep of those who have in their hearts fear of God and a good conscience, and who will never be awakened from their slumber by the black spider, but only by the friendly sun. For where such a serene spirit is present, the spider may not move, either by day or by night. But what power the spider has when men's spirits change is known only to Him Who knows everything and allots His strength to each and all, to spiders and to mankind.

ONEWORLD CLASSICS

ONEWORLD CLASSICS aims to publish mainstream and lesser-known European classics in an innovative and striking way, while employing the highest editorial and production standards. By way of a unique approach the range offers much more, both visually and textually, than readers have come to expect from contemporary classics publishing.

~

To order any of our titles and for up-to-date information about our current and forthcoming publications, please visit our website on:

www.oneworldclassics.com